FIT THE CRIME

The Inevitable Lie

BOOK 4

CORINNE ARROWOOD

TABLE OF CONTENTS

A Special Note

The statistics of PTSD are staggering. Many of our Marines and soldiers come home entrenched in the horrors they experienced and the nightmares they cannot escape. If you know one of our heroes that might be suffering from PTSD, contact Wounded Warrior Project, National Center for PTSD, VA Caregiver Support Line at 888-823-7458.

The Inevitable Lie

UNITED STATES
MARINE CORPS

CHANGE OF PLAN

With the thunderous roar of a rocket launch, his mind ventured into the dark abyss surrounded by narrative pulsating voices taunting him. *Babe, I'm pregnant. Civilian life is not for everyone, Vicarelli. We trained you to be a killing machine. With your disorder, you cannot feel; you are void of emotion, void of emotion. Trinity, I kill, kill, kill people. I'm a blight on humanity. Babe, I'm pregnant, pregnant, pregnant* echoed as though spoken into a cavern. The words hurled through like at the end of a radio ad—speedy, blurred, yet each word complete if one were to slow the velocity. The emotions zooming through his heart were a combination of shock, disbelief, happiness, anger, fuckin' scared, and full of love. He wasn't angry with her; he remembered all too well the amorous interlude where she brought up they hadn't used protection, which wasn't the only time, but rarely, perhaps less than a handful of times. He hadn't given it a second thought.

His face felt like a painted-on mask. He hadn't changed his expression, and his smile remained following his exclamation of Fuckin-A. Fingers snapped in front of his face. "Hey, boy, you still in there? You've gone to some dreamland. The family knows already. I wanted to tell you first, but I was trying on a bridesmaid dress when Bethany and Mama saw me undress. Women notice those things faster than men. No shit, huh? I all but had to draw you a picture," she snickered, shaking her head and rolling her eyes.

Standing motionless, he asked, "And your father? What did he say?"

Suddenly, he felt like a bad little boy, ready to be put in the corner or beaten. "I'm sure he's pissed and wonders what I was thinking. How irresponsible of me." He closed his eyes and rubbed his temples.

A single tear trickled down her cheek. She stood closer to him, looking up, "Given the wedding bands, he suspected we had a rushed marriage for a reason. I told him we hadn't done the I do part yet; you wanted to talk with him first. Are you mad at me?"

Babe wrapped his arms around her and whispered in her ear that he wasn't angry but shocked. He assured her he was happy. Pregnancy and babies hadn't been on his radar. Inwardly, he feared he might replicate his dysfunction. What was it Trinity had said? He wasn't his dad just as much as she wasn't hers, but what if?

Now more than ever, he needed to meet Mays Connolly, his brother. "Trinity, I'm excited but scared shitless. I don't know the first thing about babies or being a dad." He ran his hand down his face. She could see the wheels turning in his mind.

With a sassy expression, her lips slightly curled, hand on her hip, she argued, "The hell you say! You are going to be a great dad; look how much Reg, Chris, and now Jacob respect you. You're da bomb! A real-life hero, ma man."

Then, it dawned on him when Glenn had asked about Trinity; his question pertained to the baby on the way. His next move was to visit Antoine. If the man wanted to, he'd let him pulverize him and not fight back. He could certainly understand if he was pissed. After a conversation with her father, providing the answer was a thumbs-up about a wedding; he'd head to the jeweler and tell the old guy a rush would be in order. Whatever Trinity and her parents expected from him, he would comply. Things had taken a side spin, and all he knew was to hold on tight. It was a ride he never expected, thought about, or maybe even wanted, but he'd make it a good thing come hell or high water.

"I need to call your father." He nodded and spoke with what she interpreted as an embarrassed tenor, hardly his norm. Trinity watched him; he was pacing like a confined circus animal waiting for the tamer to let him out. His thoughts were all over the place, she could tell.

She grabbed his hand and pulled him into the bedroom. "Sit," she demanded, pointing to the bed. "Nobody blames you or is angry with you. You come across as ashamed; not at first, I thought you were happy, but now, not so much. What's going through your mind?" She stood with both hands on her hips, shoulders pinned back, and a concert-worthy drum roll vibrating her chest.

How could he possibly explain the myriad of flashing thoughts? It's as though all the possibilities and to-dos were hailing simultaneously with force. She stood between his legs, took his hand, and placed it on her belly, which covered her entire abdomen. Trinity placed his other hand on her breast. Now, he could feel and see the undeniable differences in her body. His eyes softened as he looked into hers. She climbed onto his lap. "I need to call your father. I don't want him to think I'm going to shirk my responsibilities." She handed him her cell after speaking into it, 'Siri, call Dad.'

"How's my beautiful girl?" Antoine sounded way friendlier than he'd ever heard the man speak to anyone, at least to his recollection.

"Um, sir, it's Babe. I think we need to talk; do you have any time this morning?" The big guy closed his eyes, hoping for the right words. Her dad said he had all the time required and looked forward to their conversation. Meanwhile, Trinity had her ear as close to the phone as possible. Babe wasn't about to put the phone on speaker at such a sensitive time. "Will you be available in half an hour?" Babe asked. Her father confirmed the meeting and seemed more personable than before. The Marine postulated different scenarios that might await. It ranged from walking into a bullet or a pat on the back, providing a broad landscape of possibilities.

"Okay, my girl, I need a shower; what do you say, funk-nasty? I'm covered in dried sweat from my morning run." He smiled and stood holding her like a child and kissed her abdomen. "How far along are we?"

Trinity laughed, coughing out a surprised, "We? Oh, we're twelve weeks, which means so far, so good." He placed her sitting on the bathroom vanity as he stripped and got in the shower. "You know many men have changes in their bodies as well. I wonder if you're going to get the pregnant daddy pooch." He jarred the shower door laughing, but clearing the air, he promised no progressing baby bump, or he'd work the pudge off mercilessly. The only thing getting more prominent was the swell of his heart.

As he was drying off, she scooted into the bedroom and returned with a pillow and his belt. She belted the pillow on his stomach. "What the hell? Ain't no fuckin way; the only bulge I want to see when I look down has nothing to do with my stomach." He laughed. "Thank you, crazy lady. I have never felt this happy in all my life. You bring out the child in me or the child that never had a chance to be silly and full of laughter." She grabbed him below with raised eyebrows. "Not now; gotta see your father." She pouted with an exaggerated jut of her bottom lip. "Later, maybe. I gotta go to work after seeing your pops."

Babe had no trouble navigating to Antoine's office. He remembered the way from their first encounter. "Good morning, Rose Marie. Is—"

"He's expecting you, hon, and by the way, congratulations on the marriage and baby news. Antoine is over the moon—his baby having a baby. Parents swear they don't have a favorite child, but there's nothing like the bond between Trinity and her dad." Her sparkling white teeth and hot pink lips enhanced her smile. *Nice lady.*

The door opened, and Antoine stepped out. He waved Babe into the office, then patted him on the back. *So, a pat and no bullets.* "What did you want to speak to me about, Babe?" Her dad pointed to a chair in front of his desk and then sat behind it to listen.

The Marine cleared his throat. "I hoped I could get your permission to marry your daughter, sir. The ring has been with a jeweler on Royal Street, getting either sized down or re-fashioned." He cleared his throat again like there was a perpetual frog that wouldn't go away. "My grandfather was a man of means and, upon his death, bequeathed his home and wealth to me, including my mother and grandmother's jewelry. Both women were statuesque; thus, the ring needed adjusting for tiny Trinity. Given the circumstances, I would like to get married as soon as possible if it is okay with you and her mother."

The whole time he spoke, Antoine observed his every movement. The big man was sincere, expressing graciousness and humility. "I'm glad you came to me; most young people think asking for a daughter's hand in marriage is a thing of the past. At first, when I heard about the pregnancy, I figured y'all had gone to the justice of the peace, and I admit I felt disrespected. We, her mother and I, understand the urgency of the situation. Since we were able to get the first marriage annulled, y'all can be married by a priest, not in the church due to Trinity's condition, but at a facility and if not, then our house, if you have no objection." *Who am I to object? He could easily dress me down for my thoughtlessness.*

"Sir, whatever you, your wife, and Trinity want works for me, but I'd like it soon." He did humble better than he thought he'd ever be able to do. He'd never kissed anyone's ass, but it seemed appropriate given the circumstances, and he pulled it off without a hitch.

Antoine leaned back in his chair, mentioned that his wife would handle all the particulars, and changed the subject; evidently, they sealed the deal. He was most curious about the rescue mission he'd heard whispered about between Glenn and his sons. Since Antoine had been involved in the cartel debacle and provided a clandestine airport pick up for him as well as all the shit from a rogue military-style entity, he had little backstory needing to complete the subject. His answer was concise, giving only the pertinent information to her father. "Is this going to be routine for you, or are you prepared to stay closer to home?" He peered over his glasses, which seemed to balance on the end of his nose. Babe was pretty sure there'd be no more rescue missions but wouldn't promise. "Are you planning on a honeymoon?" *It is the perfect excuse to look for Mays.*

Still sitting with a straight back and hands on his thighs, the Marine responded. "The people I did the rescue with are in it full-time, sir. I owe them one in return because they did a solid for me. Whether they call on me or not is uncertain, but they get in and get out pretty fast. Some people are so dedicated to the cause that they imbed themselves with the pedos and, for lack of a better word, entrepreneurs in sex trafficking." By observing her dad's body language and micro-expressions, Babe could tell Antoine didn't like the thought. "My plan is to stay close to home and be there for Trinity and the baby." Antoine was pleased by that response. No matter whether he was at home or traveling, he thought, *my true mission remains the same, and nothing will prevent me from taking out the trash,* as NOPD detective Max Sledge so candidly expressed. With the rash of murders by broken neck, the detectives put him at the top of their suspects, rightfully so, but it was an easy side-step. There were a host of martial arts and occupations trained in self-defense and most capable of torquing a neck. He was doing the city a favor.

Babe continued, "I don't know if Trinity has mentioned to you that I have taken on three boys, two teenagers, and a twelve-year-old. I have a caretaker at the house uptown; she is doing a fine job raising them. I would like them to be present at the wedding and, sir, there is no need to count the silverware. I've set clear and concise values. They want for nothing. I managed the first two before they were violated, but the last one resulted from an agreement with someone I know. I would call him a friend, but I have no friends," he chuckled, "except your daughter. As long as I have her, I need no one else." He saw the twinkle in the man's eye and a quick, almost undetectable, upturn of his mouth. *I hit the jackpot of approval from her old man*; he smiled inwardly at the thought. His statement was genuine and not an ounce of bullshit.

"Would next weekend work for you regarding the wedding?" Antoine asked. "It would have to be during the day because Nathan, Shep to most people, has to get back to the bar, or so he thinks. The man works his fingers to the bone and doesn't need to. Speaking of working, Trinity has agreed to give up bartending. She can't take any chances in her condition. You will need to wear a suit, and since you say you have no friends, I guess Glenn or one of my sons will stand as your best man. We'll be in touch." *Meeting over, no farewell, dismissed, or fuck you—and this is gonna be my father-in-law.*

Glenn was in the office trailer when Babe returned to the job site. He had a broad grin on his face. "Now, you can answer my question. I presume. Congratulations. You and Antoine have a good chat?" He laughed. "He's a different kind of person but loyal as a St. Bernard to his family. Some of his practices might stretch your Boy Scout rules, but he'll be good to you as long as you are good to his girl." *Boy Scout, hmm, quite the opposite.*

Babe stood beside Glenn's desk, relaxed and more candid than usual. "The news was a surprise, for sure, and now a quick wedding is in order. Do you want to be my best man? I'm lacking one." Glenn stood and patted his shoulder.

"You wouldn't rather someone you served with? Of course, it's a privilege, but I'd understand."

Babe put on his hard hat, saying, "No, sir. I want you on my six." He winked at Glenn.

"Done deal, Vicarelli. I'll get the specifics from Bethany." They walked around the construction site; the demolition crew had worked wonders and left as much as possible intact.

While Babe was paying attention to Glenn's comments and instructions, in the back of his mind, percolating was a trip to Atlanta and how he'd meet up with Mays. He couldn't blurt out, 'Heya bro.' The thought tickled his mind; there was enough time to come up with the right words. First, he needed to get Trinity onboard with a honeymoon to

Atlanta. Not very romantic. *Already starting out poorly.* He bet she'd be as curious to meet Mays. She'd seen photos of his mother and grandparents, all exceptionally tall and imposing.

His mind journeyed down the path of their baby. Would he or she be more Norse, French, or Haitian? Glenn continued speaking; Babe picked up the general gist but was preoccupied with thoughts of the future. They could stay in Trinity's apartment for a few more months but then move to Chestnut Street. His mind was a whirlwind of possibilities and uncertainties. Life was throwing one curve ball after another. Gleening enough from his and Glenn's conversation, it was time to begin his assigned role on site. Whether blowing smoke up his ass or in truth, Glenn complimented his acute attention to detail.

After a few hours, a food truck pulled up to the site. Babe wondered if it was just another stop. Had Glenn arranged it, or was it another of Antoine's business ventures? The fish sandwich was no longer enticing, and he'd stay safe with a burger and fries. He sat off to himself, a most comfortable disposition. It required no mundane conversations, prying questions, or bullshit bravado. A muscular and rough-looking woman sat next to him. She had a voice almost as deep as his. "Hi, we haven't met; my name is Markey. I do masonry work and welding." *Interesting combination,* he thought. Babe smiled and shook her hand as she put it out. "Now would be the time you say, hi, my name is—" *Look at this shit, let me eat in peace.*

"Babe Vicarelli." He answered succinctly with a nod.

"Interesting name. You a Marine? You look like it. I tried but didn't make it through boot; I have debilitating menstrual cramps." *What the fuck?* He tilted his head in acknowledgment but thought it was more like she had failed due to psychological issues. Who tells someone they meet for the first time about such personal matters? *Fucking nuts.* "What was it like, ya know, to be a Marine? Yeah, I know once a jarhead, always a jarhead, right?" He nodded, thinking, *leave me the fuck alone.* "I thought I'd be a shoo-in. I'm pretty strong for a female. How much do you lift? I bench one-fifty." She curled her arms and flexed. *Fucking wack job.* "You have a lift partner?"

"Never have. I'm a loner." *Get the hint.*

"Gotcha. Me too. Most men think I'm not interested in guys, but I like a hard dick just as much as the next girl. Being a Marine, I know you aren't offended by me saying that. Ya know, I like to fuck just to fuck; I don't need any of the I love you crap. You?" He held up his left hand. "Didn't realize, I guess I'm barking up the wrong tree. You got a great body, and I wondered what was inside those jeans. My bad." He tilted his head in disbelief. Even if he weren't with Trinity, he wouldn't tap that fucking psycho. "Good to meet you, Vicarelli." She winked at him, and did the guy nod. *Trinity's gonna love this story.* He chuckled to himself, still in utter disbelief.

Since he'd come straight from Antoine's, he didn't have Gunner with him, and a few of the men commented that they missed the pup. Babe told them Gunner would be there the following morning; he was sure the dog would gladly accept the attention and plethora of treats. The camaraderie on the job was invigorating. Mitchell, another welder, blasted his music and gyrated his head with the music. Others popped dance moves, which flashed him back to Louie's and watching Trinity. He chuckled inwardly, remembering how shocked she was when he sang to her. He'd sing to their baby and bear his soul. Bubbles instantaneously burst in his belly; maybe it was the sizzle he had missed all his life—a love like no other. He loved Trinity from the essence of his soul, but this was different.

The demons began showing up with terrible, slaying messages saying the baby, so pure and perfect, would know of the evil lurking within him and hate him for it. A slideshow of mangled Marines flashed one after the other as though it was his fault. How could pure innocence love a monster like him? He swallowed hard; it was the worst pain he'd ever felt like a two-ton gut punch only directed at his soul. Tears welled in his eyes. Glenn was on the other side of the site. Babe took the moment to escape to the office. He sat, hands holding his head. *If you exist, God, please remove these demons from me.* He thought back on the other times he had begged the God entity and how, while not realizing it at the time, everything he asked he had received. Maybe there was something to God, not just some conjured ideology, to make humanity feel better.

After composing himself, he headed back out. Glenn ran over to him, "Hey, Vic, sorry I didn't warn you about Markey. She is a fantastic welder and brick mason but weird in too many ways. I saw her spot you and knew the girl would beeline it to you. She's into men, all men, and the more muscle, the more intrigue for her." Glenn took hold of Babe's shoulder with a slight squeeze. Glenn was friendly, but he didn't need the chummy BFF interaction; he could take care of himself. The weird woman's offer certainly wasn't the first one he'd turned down.

"The chick's definitely out the box. I know why she didn't make it through boot with the Marines—Fucking off the deep end. I'm glad she has skills cause she's got not much else going for her. I've dealt with crazy before—not worried." Babe adjusted his hard hat and went back to work.

His phone dinged a text message notification.

> Trinity: How's work? My dad's visit?
> Babe: Work's good. Dad visit went fine. We're getting married not this weekend but next? Glenn is best man.
> Trinity: Why Glenn?
> Babe: Who else?
> Trinity: Got a point. Got appointment with Dr. Monroe tomorrow morning. Nine.
> Babe: K
> Trinity: I love you.
> Babe: Ditto, my girl. Gotta get back to it. When you giving notice to Shep?
> Trinity: Love you. Later. *I knew she'd put up a fight. Antoine can deal with his hard-headed daughter.*

He left work fifteen minutes early, hoping to get in to see the jeweler, and made it right in time. The old guy was at the till and looked up when the door chimed. "I was thinking about you just this afternoon. The ring is coming along nicely. Let me show you." He locked the front door, turned the sign to CLOSED, and entered the back room. He was beaming when he came out with the ring. "Well, Sonny, what do you think so far?" The ring needed some cleaning, but from what he could tell, the man had cut its design at the edge and attached a different band. "My only worry is that these outer stones might rub her middle and pinky fingers. I should have it done by next Friday." He smiled with an ear-to-ear grin. The man had worked magic. He closed all the gem-to-gem gaps in the setting, giving the ring a similar but different look. Babe thought it looked daintier and perfect for his girl.

"Great job, sir. It is beautiful. I need it and a wedding band by next Friday's close of business." Babe tipped his head almost apologetically. "We are getting married a week from Saturday," placing his hands on his hips in a most casual and relaxed manner.

"This I can do, but I didn't think there was any rush. I'll stay late if I have to. The band is easy; a blind man could do it. Diamonds?" He held the ring to the light, bearing a proud expression.

"Do what you think would look best. Plain or diamonds; I leave it up to the expert." He winked at the man and started to turn. He looked back around. "Thank you, sir. The situation has had a slight change," raising his eyebrows.

"My hearty congratulations on the nuptials and the new addition. I understand the expeditiousness. No worries, young man; all will be well." Babe liked the old guy. He had character, quick wit, and class. The man reminded him of his grandfather. The jeweler muttered as he shuffle-stepped to the front.

"I'd like to take you to lunch one day if you wouldn't mind." The man followed him to the door, unlocked it, and held it open.

"It would be my pleasure, Mr. Vicarelli." Babe apologized and said he hadn't asked the man's name. The old-timer returned to the counter and grabbed a slick, almost sheer business card. It had the feeling of quality. "I'm sorry, Mr. Vicarelli. My name is Levi Kahn, with a K, not a C."

Gurgles developed in his stomach. What were all these new sensations? Did he have the beginning of gastritis, or was this what emotions conjured? It was all bubbly without the feeling that he had to fart or was about to shit himself. Sometimes, the bowels had a mind all their own; he'd been there and done that. Dig a hole, lay some logs, or spray the sand like the devil's ass. Emotions, perhaps they were not overrated; but they sure as hell fucked with the body.

On the way to their apartment, he stopped at Louie's. Trinity was, like usual, swaying to the music and in her own little world. She turned with a sultry move and a sly teasing smile. "Checking in on my girl. You think all the jiggling around is good for you now since—"

She rolled her eyes. "Just how much time did you spend with my dad? You sound like him. I get it; you heard from him about turning in my notice. I have news for you and my father. I will work until I can't or the doctor advises. I know women who have worked a full day at nine months, went home only to end up in the hospital and delivering a healthy baby a couple of hours later. It is not my plan, but I would lose my mind staying home day in and day out." She was on a rant, and he wished he hadn't kicked that ant pile. *Fuck*.

"My girl, I'm heading home and then to Chestnut for dinner and see the boys. Your dad is fine with them coming to the wedding, by the way. I'm also inviting Ruthie; she's the closest thing to family I have besides Bjorn, and he sure as shit isn't coming from Norway. Maybe we'll go see him after our trip to Atlanta."

She hurried around the bar, wrapping her arms around him. "Sorry if I came on strong." He kissed the top of her head and said he understood, which he didn't, other than he didn't like the idea of her telling him what he could and could not do. The Marines' law and order was a different beast and could only function with precise rules of engagement for efficacy.

Gunner was under the bar and, upon hearing Babe's voice, bounded to him, wiggling from one end of his body to the other. His tail could be lethal for a man. A good wag in the balls was crippling. "Settle, Gunn." He looked at Trinity, "You spoil him. Look how undisciplined he is." She pulled his head to her and kissed him lightly.

By the time he made it to Chestnut, Ruthie was taking the pork roast out of the oven. The three boys sat at the dining table doing homework and were thrilled to see Gunner. "You bring that mongrel everywhere you go? He better not get on the furniture. Mr. Rune is probably rolling over in his grave." She clucked with dissatisfaction, which Babe found amusing. He grinned, thinking, *spunky old gal.*

"Ruthie, you got a few minutes to talk?" Babe asked as he watched her check the rice and peas. She turned the burners down and asked what they needed to talk about. "Trinity and I are getting married not this Saturday but next, and I hope you can make it. We aren't sending formal invitations; they are more personal face-to-face invitations. We will have a smattering of guests, but it would mean a lot to me if you—"

"Is it daytime or night?" She put her hand on her hip. "If it's evening, I'll need my son to drive me. I can't see so good at night anymore." She went for the plates; he reached over her and grabbed them. "Chris," she called out, "it's your turn to set the table." He heard 'yes, ma'am' filter in from the dining room. "You and Miss Trinity made a quick decision. You two haven't been dating even a year. Are you sure you wanna marry her?" He grinned and had an idea why she asked. *Is it social status, age, or difference in race?* None of those were issues to him, so she'd have to get over it.

He handed Chris the silverware as the boy came into the kitchen. "Do you not approve?" She said it was nothing like not approving, but the Noelle family might not accept—" She stumbled on her words, not wanting to offend him. *Ah, status.*

"I know about her family, and I was concerned, but they gave their blessing and seemed happy with the idea. Besides, she's carrying my baby." Her face beamed as though the sun had come from behind a cloud. "Clive is welcome to come, too, and I want the boys there. Ruthie, I need my family, and y'all are it. Trinity and I will permanently move here in the next few months. The house is certainly big enough. My room, or should I say Far's room, has that sitting room attached. We can turn it into the baby's room for the next couple of years. What do you think?" He observed her expression, trying to get a read. "You'll still have your room. We'll move Chris into a room by himself; I think the age difference and maturity require such. Reg and Jacob can share a room, leaving two spare guest rooms. I don't know why they haven't taken a room for themselves anyway."

After carving the pork roast, she called the boys, and they lined up to fix their plates. Ruthie served Babe's plate and told him to sit in the dining room. The dinner was excellent, allowing him to tell the boys about the wedding. They were pumped, especially after finding out he and Trinity would move into the house permanently. There was no mention of the baby. Time would tell the story.

She cleared her throat and stood. "I hope y'all enjoyed dinner; now you boys get upstairs for showers, please. You smell worse than the hound." Ruthie waited while they cleaned their dishes and headed for the shower. "They good boys, sir. Took a bit to get them in line, but they'll do you proud, and I'll have them shined like a new mint penny for your wedding." They returned to the dining room. She sipped on her after-dinner coffee. Slowly stirring the cup, she sat pensive, holding thought. "Two things I gotta ask you. Did you have anything to do with those fellas who beat Clive? When I heard of their misfortune, your face flashed before my eyes.

Most importantly, do you think Miss Trinity will mind having another woman sleeping under your roof?" *So proper and old school,* he smiled inside.

"Hang tight." He poured his two-fingers of Glenlivet. He took a draw of the drink when he sat; she could tell he was thinking. When Babe weighed options, she'd noticed a stifled word. Finally, he spoke, "I think Trinity will enjoy having you in the house. She's a people person, a social butterfly. I have funny rules about the place like I don't want her family to know where the house is, not at first. I'm not quite sure how I'll pull that off, but I'm gonna put in the effort. About Clive, God works in mysterious ways to coin you and Trinity and take it however you want." He slyly smiled at her as he touched his glass to his lips, looking over the rim.

Thoughts tumbled through his mind. He wondered if Clive had any idea. Like so many righting the wrongs, there was no reason for a verbal confirmation. He had a mission and took it to heart. As much as he believed in enforcing the law, he wouldn't make it a single day as five-o. He hardly could claim proper protocol, nor was he willing to waste time when the solution was expedient and final.

Still drudging through his mind was the possibility of returning to the Marines, but he had given, in sorts, his word to Antoine about being around for his girl and not doing the vanishing act. He tapped his finger on the table as confused thoughts linked in tandem, creating complexities. *Prioritize.* The first item on the agenda was getting Trinity to set an appointment with Mays. What would the pretense be?

All the other to-dos were mere boxes to check off—picking up the ring on Friday, getting married on Saturday, taking off to Atlanta, and maybe Narvik. His plans to engage Mays had to be precise for a true understanding of his character, and he'd judge the necessity of revealing the nature of the meeting.

"Babe, I watch you sometimes, and it's like you go to some faraway place. Whatever is playing with your mind, you need to let it go. Clive used to have that glazed-over eyes look, but it went away after a couple of years. Maybe when the baby is born, your mind will be consumed with thoughts of the precious treasure. God is good." She took the last sip of her coffee. She had a schedule to keep and had spent enough time watching him stare into the abyss; besides, he needed to get back to Trinity.

"I'll be heading out, but, as a side note, I've always been a contemplative person without the need to vocalize my thoughts. Dinner was great. Thank you." Despite the sound of her clearing her throat, he ran up the stairs and bid farewell to the boys, saying he'd see them soon. "Come on, Gunn."

"Good night, honey." She called as she climbed the steps.

CRYSTAL BALL

*I*f only a crystal ball could show him the outcome of his decisions. Babe knew the right thing was to marry Trinity, and perhaps he could have a real family for once in his life. He had to admit, even though they were a handful, he had a strong attachment to the boys, maybe feelings? *Feelings, what an odd element to life.* Perhaps a call to Dr. Schroeder, the psychiatrist he knew best, might be in order to show him sometimes the psych community was wrong. He was proof in the pudding. Quite often, the medical or psychiatric docs made mistakes in diagnosing patients as sociopaths or psychopaths; maybe they were not crazy, just people with so much hurt, causing the heart to spin layers around it as protection. *If one didn't feel,* he speculated, *then one couldn't get hurt.* Keeping it all physical, cut and dry, was much easier than exposing what lay beneath with probes into emotion and the soul. He'd need to look more into the God thing.

Babe found a parking spot close to Louie's. His girl was doing her thing behind the bar with Finn; however, he noticed she was no longer dancing on top of the bar. *Good thing,* he thought, *such action would result in a firm N-O.* She reserved his seat, still creating a swell of humor in his gut. Ruthie's comment about them not dating for a year had a reverse reaction. They had been an item for a long time. His longest relationship before Trinity was maybe a half hour, even though he paid for an hour. That was not true, he considered; the date with Denise lasted three hours, with furniture shopping, dinner, and a quick roll on his newly purchased sofa.

He sketched the timeline as he watched her mix drinks and horse around with Finn. The separation from the Corps was mid-January; the lease started in January, even though she prorated it, and here it was the end of October. The thing was, he didn't start talking to Trinity until April, but the magnetic appeal began in February. He'd heard couples talk about their dating anniversary. When would their dating anniversary be? The night she made him speak to her, or the night he gave his phone number to her, coincidentally the first night they spent together. After too much contemplation, he'd pick a date, April fifteenth, Uncle Sam's special day, easy to remember.

"Boy, where's your head at? You got that stare going. Don't you go freakin' out in Louie's." *Is that what she called it, freaking out?* The girl had no idea of the hell he'd experienced. Her horrendous episode with her ex-brother-in-law was one horrific, brutal night. Eleven years, numerous deployments, countless missions, and the rule of survival of the fittest yielded a ton of nightmares to revisit. He didn't plan them, except the one time he tried to invite them all and battle the demons from existence. *Attempt failed; maybe he nixed one or two, but that was it.*

She couldn't understand; no point in getting pissed about it. "I was trying to figure out our dating anniversary. I tried laying down a timeline but was unsuccessful, resulting in a skewed date, so I picked one."

Her eyebrows shot up with a sassy smile, "April fifth, but I started lusting for you before Mardi Gras." She winked at him. "The first time I saw you." She went back to work with a gutsy laugh, looking over her shoulder at him.

Babe saw as Trey and Max entered Louie's. They took the seats next to him. Max asked, "So, how'd it go with Bryan Bell? Stand up guy; I thought y'all would mesh."

Babe nodded, took a sip of his Glenlivet, and spoke to Max, "He introduced me to the man I needed to meet, and we had a successful mission. Thank you." He then leaned forward and spoke to Trey. "Y'all ratting the streets?" The big guy looked at Trinity and then at Trey, "How's your missus?"

Trey put his finger up to get Trinity's attention. Within seconds, she took their order. "Bourbon neat for you, Trey, and a draft, Max?" She turned and hurried away.

Babe ran his finger around the rim of his drink. Trey responded that Stephanie was well, the pregnancy was moving along, and she any day due to deliver their baby girl, Presley Jane. He looked like his buttons were about to burst as his eyes lit up excitedly. "Two blocks from here, three men held a couple at gunpoint. They pistol-whipped the woman with a couple of good whacks in the head and shot the man. I think he's gonna make it. Fuckers took her wedding ring, purse, and his watch. It's the fourth time in three weeks. We have extra patrol, but it's a crap shoot, ya know. Gotta be at the right place at the right time." Trinity handed them their beverages. "Here's to catching those cretins." *Cretins, hmm, new descriptive word. Motherfuckers rolls off the tongue like music and feels good, besides.*

"True. I'll keep my eyes open and call you if I see anything suspicious." *No, if I see the motherfuckers; their next stop will be the morgue.* Trey described the criminals as one white guy in his early twenties and two Hispanics, probably the same age. The thugs targeted couples.

Max was keen to hear information about the abducted kids. Babe gave broad strokes. He didn't divulge the rescue location and who the man's contact was, but Max grabbed the concept that the group was a team of badass warriors, and he imagined Babe fit right in. The big guy played with the idea of telling the detectives that he and Trinity were getting married but held back. It was good that Trinity had given life to his feelings, but he needed to ensure her chattiness wasn't infectious. The truth was he liked watching people, not necessarily talking with them. Babe enjoyed his internal debates; it was when he did his best puzzle-solving.

Max continued, "Now that we got some decent weather, people are coming out more at night since the humidity is lower. It also brings the degenerates out as well." The three of them watched Trinity and Finn tossing bottles to each other with choreographed panache. "That girl of yours is something else, and the kid, Finn, he seems like good-people," Babe commented he was. They left after finishing their drinks; he figured they were heading home.

Interesting, he thought, *more ne're-do-wells. I'm not going to hunt them; if it's meant to be, I'll run into them.* It was time to call it a night. The morning would come too soon. He pointed to her and beckoned with a curled finger. "I'm leaving. Call if you need me. You rocked the place tonight."

Babe looked forward to the following day. While he felt Glenn would've been cool with him going to the doctor's visit with Trinity, he'd been so on the fly that he decided to hang tight and let her come to the site with information. His morning was routine: workout, run, return to the apartment, and shower before going to work.

As he returned, he could hear her stirring in the bedroom. The door was closed, so he lightly knocked. "Trinity?" He heard her sniffle. "Trinity, are you okay?" The sniffles turned into sobs. "What's wrong?"

She folded into his arms. "I have cramps, and that's how it was when I lost the pregnancy, ya know when I was younger. I'm scared to go to the doctor. I don't want to hear that I've miscarried again." He held her; there was nothing else he could do. He didn't know enough about the whole pregnancy thing to comment.

"How about I go with you to the doctor before work? I'll call Glenn."

"Do you mind?" She sniffled again, wiping her nose on her tee shirt. Babe pulled her to him.

He moved her hair from her face. "I think we're in this together, yes?" She nodded, but the sparkle wasn't there. She was scared, and he felt helpless, a whole new feeling and one he did not like. He called Glenn. "Hey, today is Trinity's doctor's appoint—"

"Absolutely, you need to go. See you after the doc. Good luck."

Trinity dressed in her stretchy pants. Looking at her, he couldn't believe he hadn't noticed. The bump was more than apparent. The doctor's office was by Touro Hospital. Babe held her hand as they entered the office.

Baby, pregnancy, and birthing were all new to him. He grabbed every pamphlet at the reception desk, coiled them, and shoved them into his back pocket. She had to pee in a cup, weigh, and wait for what seemed forever in the room with the stirrup bed. It would feel weird having some man looking at her down there. The thought had never even crossed his mind before; there had been no reason. Dr. Cynthia Monroe entered the examination room. *Good, a woman*, he thought. *Otherwise, it might have felt awkward.*

"So, how's it going?" Trinity started to cry and explained about the cramps. The doctor allayed her fears, saying it had to do with ligaments. She gave her a handout of stretches with pictured details and instructions. When she did the ultrasound and he heard the baby's heartbeat, it took everything he had to swallow the non-stop lump coming from his heart to his throat. "Well, Trinity, it looks like the baby is developing fine and has a strong, healthy heartbeat." She turned to Babe. "We haven't met, but am I right in assuming you're the proud poppa? I'm Doctor Monroe. Your sweet lady and growing baby are doing fine."

"Babe Vicarelli and yes, ma'am. Thank you, ma'am." What else could he say? The machine printed out pictures of what looked like an alien, but he could tell it was a baby, a weird-looking one. "This is what it should look like, right?" She smiled and said yes and told them that on their next visit in a month, they could find out the gender. *Hmm. Gender? That's probably what most people think about, and it wasn't a thought at all. What if it's a girl? I don't know anything about girls, hell, or babies, for that matter. Well, fuck me running. Research time.*

In microseconds, Trinity went from tears to giggles, no sparkle to full-blown-in-your-face sparkle. His emotions, which he supposedly couldn't have, were all over the place. *What do you say now, doctors? I most certainly have fervent, burning, and intense passion. Can you feel me now, you pseudo-intellectuals?* This day had been the weirdest experience, and he'd seen much of what life offered. It was a good and scary kind of day.

His girl was back to her playful, high-spirited self.

After dropping his lady at the apartment, he went to work. "Lemme see?" Glenn asked excitedly.

"The baby looks like an alien, but the doctor said it was normal. I dunno about that?" He handed the picture to Glenn. "They gave us a whole string of them, but Trinity gave me this one for my wallet." Glenn had a wide grin, looking at the printout. "Does Bethany want children? Creating a baby has been a total shock to me; no shit, huh? You know much about babies and pregnancies?" Babe took the picture back and examined it again, pulling the pamphlets out of his back pocket. One had drawings with bulleted info regarding the progress of each month. The twelve-week cartoonish sketch looked identical to the printout. Both men studied the brochures at length. "I've taken too much time already. I'll leave them here if that's okay."

Looking with loving eyes, Glenn glanced his way. "I hope we'll have a baby soon. Bethany isn't as young as Trinity; as they say, her biological clock is ticking. It'll be baby-making time after our wedding, which is now at the top of the agenda. Gotta make a cousin for your little one; all the others are older. Although, the Noelle's breed like rabbits." He chuckled as Babe exited the office. There had been quite a few kids at the barbecue on Abduction Sunday. The backyard teemed with kids from twelve to five; the teenagers hung in the game room playing pool and watching TV. Babe enjoyed observing them, not imagining he'd have one for himself, a surprise nowhere near his radar. As far as he was concerned, he and Trinity merely enjoyed the fruits of their bodies, but someone else had other ideas. Perhaps it had been the God entity. In the past, he'd heard people say God had a sense of humor—a statement Babe now took to heart.

It was good that it was Friday because he had a challenging time focusing on anything. Babe found his mind drifting to the possibilities. Would their child be big or small, dark or fair, quiet or extraverted? The thoughts became endless and unanswerable. By his calculations, their child would be born in April, but he wasn't sure how the pregnancy calendar coincided with the actual one.

The job was moving along with demolition complete and the foundation underway. Babe looked out the fence and watched a trio of guys stroll by the site. *Hmm, one white and two Hispanic, I wonder.* An hour until knockoff, the creeps would be long gone. It wasn't his battle to fight; he had work to do, carry his weight.

Some might call him a vigilante; he'd bet the farm Trey and Max would deem it so and arrest him. Even though far from the truth, he loved that Trinity called him a superhero. *Hardly.* Javier pegged it correctly; he was a serial killer. Such a description felt cold, callous, and lacking in humanity. *Face it,* he thought; *it smacks of truth.* In the recoils of his mind, he created a school scenario, the teacher asking a bright young boy, "And little boy, what does your daddy do?" The innocent answer echoed, "He's a serial killer, but only of bad people." Did it make a difference who he'd exterminated? Could he somehow justify it in his mind? *I'm growing a fucking conscience and a berating one at that.*

Of all the lives taken and people punished, there had only been three he'd felt wrong about: Yuhn, Texas, and Ingram. In reality, most of the rogue squad thought they were advancing a rescue and deceived by the Commander, but the situation was either them or him—and he did what came naturally. *Point made; it's what came naturally.*

"Vicarelli," Glenn shouted. "It's knockoff time; it looks like your girl passed on the pregnancy fog," and he grinned. "Hey man, I don't blame you one bit. I'd be on cloud nine, too."

The two men walked side by side, going into the office. Babe picked up the pamphlets, rolled them, and tucked the wrinkled cone of paper into his pocket. "Hey, boss, I was talking with Trey and Max, two NOPD detectives, and they are looking for a trio, one white, two Latino. These sons-of-bitches have been robbing people—pistol-whipped some lady last night and shot her husband. I told them I'd be on the lookout. You'd be another set of eyes."

Glenn secured the site looking at Babe, "You're a fuckin Boy Scout, Vic. But I'll keep an eye out."

Boy Scout, my ass. "Thanks, I know they'd appreciate it. Going to see my girl."

I DO TOO

It was good to see her smiling face. She looked like the energizer bunny, flitting from one project to another, hardly taking time to give him a kiss. "Trinity, slow your ass down. Take a minute; Finn can handle the light crowd. I've been reading this," he handed her the pamphlet, "See, our baby looks just like the picture. It details the development."

She pulled out her phone. "We'll set this up on your phone; it's an app; check it out." The screen had the date and, in bold type, said, YOUR BABY IS 2.13 INCHES LONG, WEIGHS 2.05 OUNCES AND IS THE SIZE OF A LIME. YOU ARE 11 WEEKS 6 DAYS. DUE DATE: MARCH 23. In addition to the highlighted information were all the progress facts, like they could open and close their hands, curl their toes, and stuff about the intestines, which he was good not reading. He picked up a lime and looked at it contemplatively, then glanced at the printout of the alien.

"All the parts fit in the size of a lime. Remarkable." His brows furrowed as he contemplated the mystery of gestation.

She hugged his arm tight. "It's unbelievable. How can people not believe in God? He or she already has tiny fingers and toes, a perfect little person. I know we have oodles of time, but if the baby is a boy, will you want to name him after you? Do you mind if I hyphenate my name when we get married?" All these things rattled inside her brain. As far as he was concerned, her name was hers. If she wanted to take his last name, he'd go along with it, but he preferred not. He should have changed his last name years before severing ties to Gino Vicarelli.

"No way do I want to stick a child with my name." He looked her directly in the eyes with no question. His answer was definite. "Do you know the grief that came with it? Good thing I was a big kid, but if we have a boy who takes after you, he'll get the shit beat out of him every day. Trinity, you can name the baby whatever you want, as long as it's not my name. What is an oodle, by the way?" He left the God issue for another time.

Trinity responded, teasing him, "An oodle? You know, an oodle like lots of."

He nodded, remarking that it wasn't a military term he was familiar with. "Oodle? I can visualize telling my team, 'Y'all have oodles of time, take a load off.'" His chuckle was from his throat like a low rumble of distant thunder. "What is the plan for the weekend? Maybe we can take the boys and get suits for the wedding or at least sports coats, but I'd rather have suits. Your dad made a point telling me I had to wear a suit like I was some ape that didn't have any couth or social graces." He closed his eyes and slowly shook his head. "I'll tell Ruthie the boys will be with us on Saturday and Sunday. She can spend the day with Clive, which I think would help them both." A distant gaze formed in his eyes; she wasn't sure where his mind went, but it looked like happy thoughts. His mouth ticked upward on one side. "What say you, give me a quick kiss? I gotta check on the boys, but I'll be back," imitating the Terminator.

Trinity turned abruptly, "You know that's what some of the old-timers call you; it's The Terminator or The Hulk. Vicarelli, I know you told Auntie Inez, Big Paul, and the cowboy crew to make sure I didn't witness anything. Don't forget I saw you with Philip, Joey's brother. I know you are one slick, mean motherfucker." She put her hand over her mouth. "I tell ya, Vic, I been spendin' way too much time with you. I sound like a fuckin' jarhead." She couldn't keep a straight face, and even he had laughter that brought on tears.

"Oh, my girl. Now, what would Daddy say hearing you talk like a Marine? He might actually spank your ass. According to sources I won't reveal, you are his favorite. Is it because you're the most like him?" She giggled and responded no. "I'm off; see you later." He kissed the top of her head.

The truck roared with veracity. Because of all the one-way-the-wrong-way streets, Babe had to go a couple of blocks down and around to get to St. Charles Avenue. In the stop-and-go traffic, it gave him time to watch the passers-by. He saw the three from the morning, but they had picked up a couple of tag-a-longs.

He still had the Commander's locator tag from Big Paul's truck during the battle at Inez's farm. An idea popped into his head. He parked the two-fifty, got out, and followed the group of five. From posture and animation, he deduced the taller blond-haired white man was the supposed leader of the badasses. Babe caught up to them on the other side of the street. He went a few more car lengths, crossed over, pretending to glance at the phone, and plowed into him. The man's instinct was to buck up to the invader of his space, but seeing the size of the intruder, he decided to let it go and grunted.

"Sorry, sir." Babe apologized. He had dropped the tag in the pocket of the guy's sweatshirt. Up close, it was apparent the man was older than the detectives mentioned, maybe in his late twenties or early thirties. Old enough to know he was dancing with the law and the difference between right and wrong. He was a bully, and if there was one thing Babe detested, it was bullies.

"Watch where you're going, asshole." Babe put his hands up like he was backing off. He leaned against the wall and made a call, continuing the pretense. Babe reminded himself that the man pistol-whipped a woman. His only options were to detain for the cops or eliminate the threat. If the guy didn't hesitate to bash the woman and shoot the man, he was the kind that would have no problem taking someone out. The story Babe formulated in his mind made the decision lean farther toward elimination. He'd have to turn the man's gun, leaving no DNA or witnesses. The retaliation deserved more thought. He couldn't be sloppy or half-assed.

"Hey, oodles, what're you doing answering your phone behind the bar? I thought Shep shut that shit down because of Goldie Locks. How's our lime doing?" She snickered. "I love you, my girl," he quietly said. She sent a kiss through the phone with a soft, sultry love you back.

The group of five turned left down the following block, giving him an opportunity to cross over to his truck and pull out. His mind ticked over like a fine timepiece. Once he got to the house, he planned to eat and hang with the boys until it was time for them to bathe; then, he'd talk to Ruthie regarding Sunday. Given her gift of gab, enough time would have gone by to head back to the Quarter and track the guy. Hopefully, it would only be him or the three, and the tag-a-longs would be long gone. What would the plan be, then? Babe contemplated his subsequent action depending on the response from the deviants. He could plan all he wanted; whatever happened would be a responsive reaction—*thoughts over.*

The drive from the Quarter to Chestnut was becoming routine, and he felt like the truck was on autopilot. Reg and Jacob had a game of hoops going. "Where'd the basketball goal come from?" he asked, getting out of the truck.

"Clive, Miss Ruthie's son. He said every boy should have one. Can you play? I bet being so tall, it's a no-brainer for you." They bounced the ball back and forth and took shots, mostly hitting the rim and yelling brick amidst their howling.

"I played during gym class in high school, but that was it. My sport was wrestling. Pass the ball." Babe's eyes focused on the basket; he tossed the ball with a high arch, nearly making it in. "I certainly could use some practice." He took another shot and drained the net. "I'm gonna quit while I'm ahead." Reg grabbed the ball and dribbled toward the basket for a perfect layup. "Excellent, sport. Y'all gonna be with Trinity and me tomorrow. Have either of you ever been to a Catholic Mass?" Clear and concise no came from both. "Let me guess, Chris is at his girlfriend's?"

"Not this time. Brooke got grounded." Both boys started laughing. Babe asked what was funny. "Wanna know why she's punished? Her father caught them making out. He came home early from work. They'd be more than making out if it had been another half hour." Both found the subject hysterical.

Babe sat on the porch steps and watched as they hustled after the ball, taking wild shots, dribbling to goal for layups, and, then, started a game of HORSE. "Either of you have girlfriends?" They raised their eyebrows with wide eyes. "I'm just asking." He raised his arms at the elbows with his hands stretched open. Once again, the answer was a resounding no. "Good." He got up and went into the house.

Ruthie was busy in the kitchen and asked him about the basketball setup. Did he mind? The house had more life than it had had in years or maybe even ever. He had no problem at all; in fact, he was happy. Given their rough beginning, he wanted the boys to have the most normal life possible. Babe sprung Sunday church on her and hoped it wasn't a problem. "Trinity's family goes to the Catholic church." Ruthie covered her mouth and giggled, saying the boys would have no idea what to do. She was delighted to have some time with Clive. There was no doubt the old gal had her suspicions about the demise of the three street rats who beat the crap out of him. The subject never came up again since her question.

After dinner, waiting for dessert, Babe told the boys about shopping on Saturday and the plans for Sunday. The response was no more than a shrug of the shoulder, but when they found out they'd be wearing suits, all three hung their heads like they were going to the gallows.

"If I have to wear a suit, then you little," he glanced at Ruthie, who had a pensive stare looking straight at him as she entered the room with a pie, "guys are wearing suits too." They all knew what almost came out his mouth, the boys holding back their amusement. With everything said and plans made, he drove back to the French Quarter.

Playing in the corners of his mind were the three thugs and how he could eliminate them unnoticed. Most occurrences happened organically; they just happened without a plan. Babe had to plan The Commander's execution out of necessity. The memories of his other eliminations began to ignite in his mind, like popcorn at the theater. It made an interesting montage. A slight upward turn of his lips formed. He had executed everything to perfection; his chest rose with exaggerated breaths of pride. His most titillating was hands-on, period. Babe made his decision; it would have to happen in the moment and not set up. That's why his other encounters worked well; no room for deliberation. It was them or him. There was a definite fluidity to his method. Hearing about it and seeing the actual pieces of shit in the act were two totally different things. His body's response made it evident that the heat of the moment was exhilarating and powerful, complete with increased respirations, a bounding pulse rate, and a slight discomfort in his jeans.

There would be no stalking, lying in wait, or the gnaw of anticipation. Babe parked a few blocks away and walked to Louie's. Trinity was behind the bar, and he couldn't help but notice some of her crazy dance moves had tamed. It was still entertaining, but at least to him, the wild jumping around, twerking, and rough gyrations were noticeably absent.

It would do her good to get away from it all. While Atlanta was hardly a romantic getaway, Norway was a different story. *Does she have a passport? I need to ask.* If not, that would be a huge issue; getting one issued took weeks, if not months, for civilians. The question then arose as to the validity of his Special Issuance passport. He should have turned it in upon separation from service. Norway might be on hold. *Call Daniel;* he made a mental note.

The reserved sign was in front of his seat. Trinity quickly brought his Glenlivet, grabbed his hand, and kissed the top. "Getting off at midnight. Dad told Shep about," pointing to her abdomen, "and I have reduced hours." His lady appeared a bit disgruntled, but he detected a slight twinkle of satisfaction in her eyes. *Good, time to talk tonight.* A loud thumping on the bar prompted her to say, "My cue, Vic." She looked at the guest; it was the same loudmouth from weeks before. Babe picked up on Finn's concern and put two and two together.

The big man wove through the crowd and stood directly behind the piece of shit. "Hey, you, little nigga girl, gimme a scotch and soda." Finn was on it, made the drink in record time, and put it in front of the man. "Guinea boy, I told the nigga whore to get it."

Finn smiled, "Sir, that would be Mick or Paddy, not Guinea." The man picked up the glass and started to throw it at Finn, who had already pressed the button when he saw it was the troublemaker. Babe grabbed the man's wrist before he could throw the glass, which fell from his hand onto the bar. "Get the fuck off me." The man couldn't turn as the crowd was shoulder to shoulder. He tried to pull his hand away. Babe felt the bones crack. The man cried out in pain. "You broke my fucking wrist. I'm gonna sue your ass. Do you know who I am?"

Babe leaned down and whispered, "Sue me, asshole. One more word to my woman, and I'll hunt you down like the animal you are, motherfucker. No need to worry about your wrist; there'll be pieces of you scattered around the city. You'll be a puzzle never solved." The man shoved back and forth, the people around him staring at the mayhem he was creating. Two uniforms entered Louie's. One had met Babe during the crazy kidnapping incident, and the NOPD officer lifted his chin and eyebrows in acknowledgment.

They made their way to the man; Babe stepped aside. The man began to rant, "This man broke my arm; I want him arrested."

"Wrist," Babe corrected, "and you did it to yourself; I just held it so you couldn't throw the glass at the bartender, much as you tried."

Shep rounded the bar and saw the man. "Mister, I told you already you are not welcome in my establishmment." Babe knew the handcuffs were gonna hurt like a mother and somehow felt content about it. The officers tried to usher the man out, and he started to fight back. Babe chuckled inside, grabbed the man's belt and shirt, moving him through the crowd. One of the officers had opened the back door of the unit. Babe sat him in the car, forgetting to push the man's head down. There was a distinct thwack when his noggin hit the top of the door frame.

He could hear the man bawling about the broken wrist and stating Babe threatened him. Nobody cared or listened. In truth, the man broke his own wrist; Babe just had a tight grip. He knew the outcome from previous encounters with self-absorbed pricks who thought they could throw objects at people.

Shep pulled Trinity aside; Babe could see her shaking her head no. The older man nodded with an undertone, and then Trinity stomped her foot and said no emphatically. Shep threw his arms in the air. The big guy knew his lady well enough that no one had to tell him what had happened. She was one hard-headed woman. *Poor Shep*.

Babe returned to his seat. Now, he knew what the offender looked like. From his dialect, one who knew the dialects and accents of different areas of the city could quickly identify where a person grew up or lived. The man was most assuredly a resident of the Garden District. Life and fate were funny things. Maybe the two would meet again; they might bump into each other when he was taking a morning run. There was no urgency in doing anything else to the sack of shit; he'd made a statement with the wrist, but people of the man's disposition thought they were above the rest, and a warning, even being a second one, would not deter him from entering Louie's again.

After a couple of hours, Trinity picked up her backpack and signaled Babe to head out. Instead, he met her at the end of the bar and escorted her out. There would be no unwanted gropes or inappropriate handsy behavior. His face was grave, without the slightest indication of a smile or friendly expression. Anyone looking at him knew the big man meant business.

Once out of Louie's and the noise had died down, he spoke. "I think I'm gonna like this midnight thing. It'll give us time to talk and—"

"Get busy," she ended his statement and giggled. "Even though I put up a fuss, I do too." She went silent for a minute. "Vic, say, I do. I want to hear how it's going to sound. My insides get all fizzy when I think of you repeating vows and saying I do. Oh, and the 'you may now kiss your bride,' it's only meant for a sweet tiny peck." He raised his eyebrows.

"What do you think I'm gonna do? Give me some credit. After the I do, it's not like I was gonna start humping you." He laughed. "You and your dad must think I don't have a brain or lack all civility. What the fuck?" He paused, turned her to face him, looked her lovingly in the eyes, and softly said, "I do."

"I do, too, Babe."

PHASE ONE READY

The thought of her getting off at midnight Tuesday through Saturday excited him. She passed the key card and unlocked the door. "I like this new schedule, Trinity. I can stay with you until quitting time every night and not worry about some creep jumping you. Am I gonna be too much of a pain in your ass? I'll still have dinner with the boys and head to Louie's for ten. How's the thought grab you?"

She danced around him as he walked to their bedroom. "This is what I want to grab," she cupped his butt. She plopped on the bed, cocking her head to one side. "What's the plan with Mays?"

Taking off his jeans, he said, "Exactly what I wanted to talk over." He carried his jeans, shirt, and her dirty laundry to the washer. He returned to the bedroom. She scoped his body, puckering her lips and running her tongue across her teeth. She let out a trilling purr. "Seriously, I think you should make an appointment to see him, and I'll be with you. I wonder what he remembers from childhood. If he remembers our grandfather, then he'll know we're related. Except for the dark hair and olive skin, I look like him. I have Gino's dark hair and olive complexion, but my mom's eyes maybe not as light, but the sperm donor had eyes of coal."

A deep soul-wrenching hollowness in the pit of his gut created waves of nausea and seething anger. Trinity watched as the redness moved from his neck to his face, and the tips of his ears turned a deep crimson. "Hey, hey, don't think about him. No point. What's done is done, and you don't have to deal with him ever again. Before you even go there, you are not; do you hear me, not like him." He slipped into the bed next to her. Trinity's eyes locked on his. Babe felt like his gut was on a seesaw, up and down, perplexed by the topsy-turvy world of feelings. He pictured his emotions like an artist's palette with a smorgasbord of colors, each representing an emotional link that could readily collide with another, forming yet another weirdness. *What would the shrinks think of me now?* It hit an odd chord with him that these untouchable, mysterious bursts could play such havoc with his physical body. Whirling between the mess of the feeling world, he realized it had been some time since he'd regularly hit the heavyweight bag; perhaps it was the missing link to his stability.

Babe kissed her forehead, got out of bed, and cruised into the living room. *And here lies another issue caused by relationships—a total upheaval of routine.* The distraction had slammed him in every aspect. He started slow with the bag, warming up, limbering his body. The pace increased, and it felt good. It was like tiny bursts of electrical forces raging in battle with the emotional world, controlling, demanding they fit in their proper place and not fly out at will. He would allow them to release but be perfectly controlled, not have random flashes like flipping a light switch on and off in a strobe-light manner.

He felt her presence when she stepped into the doorway but concentrated on his exercise. Blood coursed through his body, ramping up energy. After half an hour working out on the bag, he returned to the bedroom, guzzling a couple of bottles of water. His body, drenched in sweat, pulsed with life. He turned on the shower, stripped off his sweaty boxer briefs, and stood beneath pelting blasts of water. It was only moments later when she got in with him. Her hands reached out, holding him close. "Vic, your kicks are high. I mean, you could smack someone in the head with your foot." She stopped and thought a moment, "Have you ever done that? Never mind, I don't want to know." She nestled against him, then pulled back, looking up at him, "Would their head like fly off their body?"

Shedding water from his face with squeegee-like strokes, he said, "I thought you didn't want to know. No, they wouldn't be decapitated, but it's a good move if someone comes at you with a weapon. It keeps you from their grasp, and the outcome is determined depending on whose reflex is faster. If they have obscene skills, they can grab your foot or leg, and then you're fucked. You worried about your hair?"

With a flirty smile, she slowly turned her head back and forth. He slid her up against the stone wall. She wrapped her arms around his neck, anticipating his passion. His half-hour workout resurrected his primal desire, and he regained self-confidence, determination, and control. Vic was back to being Vic, the powerful, cagey Marine. The self-doubt, endless suppositions, and bewilderment had vanished. Sated, the bed beckoned them.

Saturday morning clambered in, and it was time to hit Perlis on Magazine Street with the boys. "Vic, you been to Domilise's? I like it as much as Mother's. Also, are you sure you want to spend that much on suits for the boys?" She dressed quickly and braided her hair down the side over her shoulder. He slowed her down.

"Girl, I'm gonna work out, so take it easy. Watch the tube or pick up a book. Relax. I also need to go to the Garden District Book Shop. I want to pick up a book on pregnancy, what to expect, and what I must be doing to prepare." She rolled her eyes at him. "Roll your eyes all you want. I like to be informed. Those pamphlets were informative but showed me how much I don't know." He lightly swatted her butt on his way to the living room. Calling back over his shoulder, "Does it look like I'm ready to go shopping?"

"Well, considering you are in your underwear, I'd have to say you're a bit underdressed." She snickered. He ignored her flippant response and proceeded with his routine.

Trinity turned on the television, but Babe's workout mesmerized her, making it impossible not to watch him. His body was strong, each muscle carved perfectly, and he was hers. After lifting, crunching, and pushups, it was time for the heavyweight bag. Amid a strike from his right foot, he folded in laughter. "This will never work. All I can picture is you asking about someone's head flying off. How can I take this seriously when you watch my every move?" Babe lifted one side of the sofa and pivoted it on an angle, putting her back to him. She rolled to her knees, propped her head on her hands, and gazed at him. "Give me twenty minutes of solitude." She turned off the television and went into the bedroom. The strenuous fight with the bag commenced. After twenty minutes, he was coated in a film of sweat, some areas running through the curves of his muscles like tributaries. He felt strong and agile as he jogged into the bedroom, "Two-minute shower, and we'll be ready to go. Good enough?"

She could hear him turn the shower on. Trinity sashayed into the bathroom. "Why don't you like me watching?" She pressed her face to the glass. "Why are you always trying to hide me from witnessing your special skills? Like at Inez's," she put on a deep tone to her voice, "Make sure Trinity doesn't see any—"

Babe interrupted, "Because I want you to forget any violence you've seen, and every time I get into full-blown mode, I can see fear in your eyes. You once said you were not afraid of me, but I can see your body saying something else when it looks like there might be a confrontation. As I told you, it scares the shit out of me at the thought of a hallucinatory conflict where I perceive you as something or someone else. I would never forgive myself if I hurt you. Workouts, especially no holds barred, have occasionally triggered illusory moments."

As promised, the shower took only a few minutes, and he dressed in no time. They set off to Chestnut Street to pick up the boys. They walked to his truck. Trinity chattered endlessly about him parking on the street, not at the hotel garage. He had no desire to feel like Freddie the Freeloader or appear to be taking advantage of the Noelle's generosity. Babe had made it clear that they would be moving uptown after a few months. He hoped it would be enough to warrant her quitting Louie's, but that was her call to make.

While Babe had worked out, she researched the firm where Mays was a partner. She added the number to her contact list. "While you were clocking someone's head off, I found the info on Mays. Monday, I will make an appointment with Lawyer Connolly for next week. The wheels are starting to move slowly." The way she said it reminded him of a train leaving the station. The movement was slight initially, but before the passengers knew it, they were speeding along the track. Dollars to donuts, it would be a similar scenario.

The boys waited on the front porch for Babe and Trinity. They furiously knocked on the window when the truck pulled into the driveway. Ruthie came out onto the porch as Babe and Trinity approached. "We'll take the sedan," he said to the household commandant, "I'll be back with the boys, but we'll bring dinner home for everyone. Trinity goes in around four. See you later."

He pulled the sedan out of the garage. Chris expounded, "This is a paw-paw car. When are you gonna sell it and get something more your speed?" Babe grumbled that he had no plans to get rid of the car, and maybe it was his speed.

For the first time, either in a long time or ever, Babe felt settled. These were his streets, and the world felt familiar. It was an odd sense of belonging. The boys had been right; with three lads that would only be getting bigger and a baby needing a car seat, he and Trinity would have to relinquish their vehicles for more appropriate family mobiles. Chris hadn't asked yet, but Babe knew it wouldn't be long before he'd want to drive. Chris was sixteen, nearing seventeen. Perhaps he should hold on to the sedan, knowing it was safe. The truck was too big for a novice to handle. When it came to the time, which was only a year away, would he recommend college or the military? Enough thoughts on the subject.

They pulled up to Perlis. The boys immediately went mute. Babe figured they must have felt overwhelmed. He felt a tickle in his throat stemming from his inner core. Was he excited about getting married? It wasn't a heightened edge like skydiving into hostile territory, wondering if you'd make it to the ground alive.

An older gentleman greeted them, learned about the reason behind their shopping endeavor, and pegged each boy's size at a glance. He knew his business and suggested two-button navy blazers with khaki pants, a button-down, and a tie. It would be the most versatile and prudent move. *Boys done.* When it came to Babe, unless he had a custom suit made, which was barely enough time, he'd have to wear his dress blues. Knowing it was within policy since it was their wedding, he somehow felt disrespectful to the Corps—*decision made, dress blues, done.*

It was barely worth driving and parking for stop two, the bookstore. "Why are we stopping here?" Reg wanted to know, wrinkling his forehead with a slight tilt of his head. The other boys hadn't spoken since trying on jackets and pants. They remained silent in the car. Trinity turned the radio up and put her window down, letting some of the tension leave the sedan. She bobbed her head and body to the beat. Babe looked at her, finding her natural rhythm amusing, if not arousing. Reg laughingly said, "Trinity, like some of the guys in the Quarter, say, 'You, go, girl!' You can dance even sitting down."

Babe glanced in the rearview mirror, "You have no idea, Reg."

"Vic, why are we going to a bookstore?"

"We're not; I am. Be right back, and then it's time for poboys." It was Chris and Jacob's first reaction since the Perlis adventure, and all three boys became rambunctious. He leaned in the window. "Don't give Trinity any shit, you hear?" She pointed at Babe as if scolding, rolling her eyes, shaking her head, but with a grin.

Through mumbles, they all said, "Yes, sir."

He was in and out of the bookstore with a quick purchase, and mere minutes later, they were walking into Domilise's, placing their order, and grabbing a table.

Trinity's impatience and excitement for Monday to roll around was infectious, and she could see Babe drumming his fingers, bouncing his knee, and almost hear the beating in his chest. She couldn't fathom having a brother and not knowing about him until adulthood. Her man had to have mixed emotions, and the poor thing had only recently discovered feelings. Since the feelings advent, Babe was in an avalanche of emotional triggers. Deep in her bones, she predicted an illusional episode was around the corner. All the stress of everything he had been through, the wedding, the baby, and now the potential of meeting his brother had to have upset the apple cart, leaving him open to vulnerability.

"Sir," Jacob asked, "Do you read a lot?"

"Some, yes." He took a bite of his sandwich.

"So, what book did you get?" Jacob was a typical inquisitive and nosy twelve-year-old. Babe felt the boy's longing for love and acceptance and looked at the big guy as his hero since being rescued by him.

"A grown-up book." Babe succinctly answered, then took a sip of his drink.

Reg challenged, "You read porn?"

Babe nearly choked on his sip and swallowed quickly. "No, sir. Where the fuck did that come from? It's a, uh—" he pleadingly looked at Trinity, who answered it was about babies. The three boys slowly looked in her direction, wide-eyed and curious.

Chris' eyes became round as saucers, "Now I understand the rushed wedding. Yes, sir."

"Not.Another.Word.Chris." Babe emphasized in a no-nonsense way, to be sure. The subject came to an abrupt halt. Not that he needed to explain himself to anyone, but he felt an explanation was in order for some stupid reason. "We were getting married anyway. Got it?"

Without hesitation, Chris quickly said, "Yes, sir."

The questions flowed freely again around the table about Trinity's parents and the wedding. Things came to light when Trinity explained that instead of going to church with Ruthie, they'd go with them and then to her parents so the boys could meet everyone before the wedding.

They all headed back to the French Quarter apartment until it was time for Trinity to go to work. She had the escort of all three boys and Babe to Louie's.

Once delivered safely to Louie's, Babe and the boys drove through Popeyes. He called Ruthie, "Ma'am, ask Clive to come for dinner. We picked up enough Popeye's to feed an army."

An hour later, Ruthie got home, and Clive followed soon after. The night was filled with conversation, watching TV, and general lazing around until it was time for the boys to go upstairs and for him to head to Louie's. Unbeknownst to Babe, soon after he left, Clive decided to meet him there.

Babe found a parking spot a few blocks away. His mind was on seeing Trinity, not on the shadows moving across the street, but his canny senses picked up a hint of danger, and like a spark to tinder, his at-the-ready was in high gear. He heard quick steps cross the street behind him, then saw a single figure cross in front of him. The two behind him came up on either side, and the one in front of him raised his arm, holding a gun. "Your watch and wallet," the man in front commanded.

"Get the fuck out of here. Don't pick a fight you can't win." Babe growled.

The man holding the gun became irritated and took a few lunging steps toward the big man in an attempt to dominate. "Stupid motherfucker I got the gun. Hand over your shit, or I shoot." He shuffled a few steps closer.

Babe lowered his head, focusing intensely ahead at the man. In a sweeping movement at blink speed, the Marine kicked the gun out of the man's hand. The other two on each side of him loosened their grip in surprise, and as he flung one to the pavement, he caught a glimpse of Clive tackling the other. He was thankful he hadn't put a boot to the man's throat, which he would have instinctively done.

Police cars screeched to a halt. Officers rushed to the scene. Between Clive and Babe, they contained the three men. As he suspected, the encounter would happen organically. It might have been more challenging, but Clive's maneuver, taking the third man out, contained the threat. The police cuffed the three just as Trey pulled up. He looked at Babe and shook his head. "Can't say I'm shocked to see you in the mix. You end up in the oddest of places. You have some kind of internal honing device. I swear, Babe."

"How's it hanging, Detective? Fancy seeing you here. As I've said before, I don't know why people want to pick a fight with me."

Babe and Clive walked over to Trey and shook the detective's hand. "I think these three might be the motherfuckers y'all been looking for from the other night. They wanted my watch and wallet and held a gun on me. I'm one lucky bastard that Clive showed up when he did. Who knows what would have happened?" *I would've killed them all*, ran through his mind. He introduced Clive to Trey and said they were heading to Louie's.

"Y'all enjoy, and I might see you later." Trey got in the car and radioed dispatch.

Clive followed Babe to Louie's. "Man, I can't believe those dudes were all over you. I hoped I could catch up with you when you left; I'm glad I hurried." He nodded as he spoke. The night's activity boosted Clive's confidence, which hadn't fully recovered from the beating he took from T-Train and his associates. Babe took a deep breath; he was back on his game.

The ramble of thoughts commenced. Why did they single him out? Their MO was couples, not big loners. Maybe their overconfidence, having three against one, made them delusional. Had Clive not stepped in, he would have crushed the guy's windpipe, struck the other in the throat with the heel of his hand, and the guy with the gun had already peed himself when the gun went off, thinking he shot himself. The asshole's plan hadn't worked, which threw him into a panic. Fear was a brutal sparring partner. It won almost every time—a total mind fuck.

"Thanks for the help. I'll buy the first round." They turned into Louie's and watched Finn and Trinity work their magic behind the bar. "That's a hot li'l thing behind the bar." Babe forgot Clive hadn't met Trinity yet. "I bet she—"

"Hold your thought. The girl's smokin', hell yes, and come Saturday, she'll be my wife." He felt for Clive; the look of shock, embarrassment, and shame culminated in wide eyes, a hitched breath, followed by a sigh. "No worries, Clive. Who would rationally think that beauty would want the likes of me? No harm; no foul, man." She had his seat reserved. She glanced over and blew him a kiss. She rushed his Glenlivet. "What do you want?" Clive answered a beer was fine. "Trinity, this is Ruthie's son, Clive. A beer for him, please." In the far corner was an empty table. He let her know they'd be sitting at a table.

As they sat, Clive offered up congratulations. "My mom told me you were getting married. She asked me to drive her. She's a hard-working woman, my mom. She loved your grandfather a lot and thought the world of him. Mom had been with an agency, sitting elderly people, but once she met your granddad, she left the agency and went full-time with him. The old gal has pepped up since the boys moved in. I know there's a story there, but she never told me anything other than you moved them into the house. She says they're good boys."

Babe touched his drink to his lips, glancing over Clive's shoulder at Trinity. "Oh, hell, no." He pushed the chair back and, with intensity, walked up to the bar. The same rude jackass was at the bar hassling Trinity. "Get the fuck out of here, motherfucker. I told you I'd kill you the next time you came here. You made the wrong decision." He had already grabbed the knife from his ankle and jabbed it into the man's side, under the rib cage, deep into the lung. Babe swiftly moved to the table.

The lung would take a few minutes to fill with blood. The man had no idea what had happened other than he was in pain and his breathing labored. With any luck, he might go into cardiac arrest. The crowd was too thick for anyone to see anything; besides, he'd been at the table with Clive. That was his story, and he was sticking to it.

The next few minutes at the bar continued with the steady interaction between Finn and Trinity, and then, as the song ended before the next one started, the sound of a woman shrieking filled the air. Shep was already through the kitchen door. Finn had pressed the button, which meant the cops would be there momentarily. "What's going on at the bar?" Clive asked.

"A crass piece of shit comes in here once in a while and harasses Trinity. The owner has to come from the back and help the police escort him out. Last time, I helped get him in the car, but it looks like the boys in blue brought reinforcements. I'll watch the show this time and sip my whiskey. Hopefully, they'll lock him away or get a court order preventing him from coming here." Clive watched as Babe explained. Whether he bought the story mattered not.

"I guess there's little chance of getting a beer with the drama. Want to go down the street?" Clive gulped the last swallow in his beer mug.

Babe looked around, trying to get Trinity's attention. He'd text her that he'd be back. Remembering how she had giggled when he impersonated The Terminator saying 'I'll be back,' brought a warmth to his heart. She could be light-hearted and childish one moment and then sultry, emanating desire and creating a hunger in him that she could only fill—a little girl and temptress all in one.

They walked halfway down the next block into the first opened door, ordered their drinks, and sat. Clive was curious, "So what is the story with the boys?" Should he go down that rabbit hole? Why not? He started the story with Trinity's horror, then went to Chop, entering Louie's. Babe skipped the details of killing the two men. "How'd you not take that piece of shit out? If he did that to your girl, it's just a matter of time before he'll get someone else."

Babe shook his head. "Not gonna happen. So, like I was saying, a helo pilot I served with shows up at Louie's, I thought he was stand-up, but he's a lying piece of crap. The truth of it, he was coming to check out Trinity since the plan to abduct her had failed. I guess trying for a second chance. Long and short, I ended up in Pensacola and caught him loading a drugged working girl and two street kids into his bird. That's how I got Chris and Reg." He sipped his drink, then continued about the snake and his abduction.

At that point, Clive spoke, "W-wait, this guy fucked you hard, and he's still walking? That's sick. I woulda taken him out, no doubt." The comment drummed memories and how, at one time, torturing Chop was the top priority. *Hmm. Maybe when we get back from finding Mays.*

PHASE TWO SET

His phone dinged.
Trinity: Where are you?
Babe: Forgot to text where we ended up
Trinity: You missed the action
Babe: Fuck, you ok?
Trinity: See you soon?
Babe: On my way.

"*C*live, thanks for your help with the attack. Much appreciated." He grabbed his arm with a shake. Closer than a handshake but less than a hug.

Both men stood. "I've been wanting to talk since getting my ass kicked. Thanks. You are one badass motherfucker. Glad you are on my side. My mom likes the kids and will be a big help when the baby comes. We gotta do this again, oh, and thanks for the wedding invite. We will be there, Mom and I."

The police had wrapped crime tape around Louie's. If he had to bet, he was confident Shep was not pleased. *My bad.* Trinity was sitting in one of the chairs at a table. "Vic, you missed the excitement." She was jiggling in her chair, full of animation. "Remember that racist jerk?" Babe nodded. "He started shit at the bar. Customers were shoulder to shoulder; Finn and I worked our asses off. Then, the guy gets all weird with bug eyes, gasping for breath and grabbing his chest. I've never seen such fear. He was shittin' on himself. He collapsed against one of the regulars, who pushed him back. Some lady screams that he's bleeding. I think he's choking on his rude words. The guy died. He had a pneumo-something that led to a heart attack. The police tell Shep the guy was shivved right here at our bar. It must have happened before he came here because we had a nice crowd of well-behaved people. I saw you and Ruthie's son sitting at the table, and the next thing, y'all were gone. The police have the recording from tonight." *They have me at the bar.*

Babe listened attentively. "Trinity, you don't remember me coming to tell you we were leaving. It was too loud to talk."

She cocked her head, "I woulda remembered that you are a pretty massive customer to forget. Besides, I always remember the handsome ones. No, I don't remember, duh, that's why I texted you." She turned her hands up.

"C'mon, let's get home. You good to leave?" Babe questioned.

She answered with a touch of attitude, "I've been ready to leave. Finn's gone, the bussers are gone, Shep is in the back, very disgruntled. I gotta let him know we're leaving."

They waited while he locked the place up, and they left together.

Once in the truck, she began drilling him about Clive. He still had signs of being in a nasty fight, which made her most curious. When Babe told the story, she put her hand to her mouth. "Ruthie must have been devastated. What happened to the guys who beat him up? Did the police get them?"

Looking straight ahead without an inflection in his tone, he calmly answered, "They picked the wrong man to attack and met an early demise, from what I heard." She commented there should be a lot more justice like that, and maybe the crime in the city wouldn't be as rampant. "My thoughts exactly." End of conversation regarding crime.

They talked about taking the boys to church with her family and then to her parent's house for dinner. He imagined her mother, Bethany, and Trinity would be planning the staging of the yard and the house for the big day. It was Trinity's idea to get married at the family home. Babe hadn't disclosed he'd be in uniform. She'd never seen him in dress blues and hoped it would be acceptable. "I have someone I'd like to invite; is that okay?" He wouldn't be the only one in dress blues if Coach Kennedy could make it. Babe tried to estimate how old the man would be, maybe in his late sixties. In all those years, they never discussed Coach's age, family, or Babe's home life. Coach had jawed about the Marines, a little about his service; all the while, Babe listened silently; his silence spoke volumes.

She held his hand and watched him, "Of course, invite anyone you want." Being with him woke butterflies in her stomach and aching to be in his arms. In slight trickles, tears rolled from her eyes.

There was no need to glance over; he could feel the warmth emanating from her. With a slight tilt, he saw the tears, his emotions gathering in a knot in his throat. He could tell hers were happy tears that ignited sensations throughout his body. The blood moved through him as though he could feel the speed of its motion. *Is this what other people feel?* He thought. If so, he had missed out on the emotion department, explaining why he didn't know what to do with the tiny fireworks popping in his gut. Perhaps it was all confusing, but at least he wasn't numb or void like most of his life. *Thank you, Trinity.*

Babe woke with the birds tiptoeing out of the house, stretching for his run, and took off. The sunrise was magnificent. *God's handiwork? That's what Trinity said.* He had started to warm to the idea of God, especially upon hearing the baby's heartbeat. The glory of it all caused him to stop allowing the moment to engulf him and then pressed Coach Kennedy's number. Even though it was early, Coach was one of the reasons Babe started morning runs.

"Only one person I know would call at such an obscene time. Doesn't the sunrise leave you speechless, Vicarelli? Of course, that isn't saying much with you," and he chuckled.

"Good morning to you, too, sir. How are you? Before we go any further, would you consider attending my wedding this Saturday?" A dribble of sweat ran down his neck.

A loud sigh came from the other side of the phone. "No shit, Vicarelli. Want me in my dress blues?" His voice was still boisterous with the gravel like many of his commanding officers. He barked the same, causing a quickening, and it felt good.

"Yes, sir. I won't stand out as much or feel as conspicuous." Babe waited for some smart-ass remark.

"Marine, you and your honey are in the spotlight. Get the fuck over yourself. By the way, you still in?"

Babe moved dirt around on the sidewalk with his foot. "No, sir. Separated about ten months ago. It was time. You are gonna like my girl, Trinity. Coach, she's got a heart of gold and is the sweetest yet feistiest thing on two legs. You won't believe it when you see her. It doesn't get more beautiful than her."

The coach started talking and said he could tell it was the real deal; he'd never heard him speak so much during their friendship, at least not with emotion. After giving all the pertinent information, like the date, time, and address, Babe asked if they could get together. "I hear much growth in your voice, son. I remember you in my prayers every night. Happy for you, Vic. I know the Corps was your mistress for a long time, but now it sounds like you found someone to hug you back. I'll see you on Saturday now finish your run."

Yes, he thought, if ever there was someone he wanted at the wedding, it was Coach. If what Trinity said was true, then his grandparents and mother would be watching over him; their spirits would be in attendance. It made him feel peaceful, but then the voices said that was the purpose of the made-up heaven and only fools ran after such preposterous thoughts.

The internal debate began, and he was determined to believe Trinity's story. *Fuck the negative voices.* He pushed hard to get back early enough to shower with his woman and see if anything rose to the occasion.

Babe made it in time to jump in the shower before she got out. The whole house was buzzing with excitement. The boys were dressed, had finished breakfast, and played a video game while they waited for the adults.

There were just the five of them in the house. Trinity instructed all three to be on their best behavior. Her eyes shifted to Babe as if to say, "That means you, too." The boys chattered the whole way to St. Dominic's Church. Questions popped up asking what her parents were like. The big guy cleared his throat, looking in the rearview mirror, "Trinity's parents are Mr. and Mrs. Noelle, and you address them as such. Make sure to say yes, not yeah, and stay on top of your ma'ams and sirs. We square? Any questions?" They were curious about the kids. "You'll do fine; be yourselves without the four-letter words, even if they use them. Got it?"

In unison, they answered, "Yes, sir."

Traffic was light, and they made it to St. Dominic's early, gathered, and waited for her family. He could see the nervousness in their silence. The first to arrive were her parents. *Perfect.* He had hoped they could have a moment with the kids before the others arrived. All three boys excelled in politeness and speaking with her parents. He could tell Antoine was amused by them. They came across as three average kids, well-groomed and assured. Babe didn't hear what Reg said to her mom, but Antoine chuckled, and her mom smiled warmly, thanking Reg for whatever he said. Out of the three of them, Reg was the schmoozer. He knew when to bat his eyes, put on a look of innocence, and was quick on his feet to respond appropriately.

The next five minutes were filled with introductions as her brothers arrived with their children. Bethany and Glenn showed up in time to grab a seat with the family. Trinity sat beside her dad, the three boys beside her, and Babe at the end. He saw how her dad kept a close eye on the boys. He guessed the man was sizing up the job Babe had done with them and telltale perhaps of his readiness for a new little one. Babe drew a slow, deep breath; this was his new reality. There were no bubbles of intensity or knots concerning disapproval, and when did he even start giving a shit? His pulse was steady and relaxed. Even though the boys hadn't attended a Catholic Mass, they handled themselves perfectly. For Communion, Trinity told them to cross their arms in front of their chests, and they would receive a blessing from the priest. *Step one done*, he smiled inwardly.

The drive to Swan Street included non-stop questions about their new cousins. Chris asked if they'd be cousins. Before Babe could answer, Trinity said yes. There was no awkwardness when they arrived, and the boys played together like they'd been family all along. The only odd man out was Babe. Socializing was not his gift; he remained quiet, observing all the activity. Not much got past the big guy; it was what the Marines expected from him.

Antoine Sr. cornered him, "Marine, you said these kids came off the streets. You have done a fine job with them. Nobody would ever know. Those kids are well-mannered—"

Babe interrupted, "They better be. The lady who manages my home is loving but strict. She dresses me down sometimes. I find it amusing but perfect for three boys who have seen life's rougher side."

Like meals on Chestnut Street, Mrs. Noelle and the girls set dinner buffet style. From Ruthie's firm instruction with the boys, they knew precisely how to act and serve themselves. The kids sat at a table outside by the pool. Babe was waiting to see if any of Trinity's sibling's children inquired where the boys came from, and either they were told not to, or it didn't cross their minds; no one ventured there. All the adults knew part of their story.

Trinity was doing her thing, flitting around. He sat and watched. Chance sat in the chair beside him, chomping at the bit to engage. "The buzz in the family is that you went on a rescue mission to free trafficked kids. Is that true? You had to be shitting yourself. That's cartel stuff, right?"

"Yes, it was intense, but ended with success." Babe took a bite of food as though punctuating the conclusion of the conversation; however, like Trinity, Chance could talk and drilled him with questions. Without being rude, the big guy explained that the operations were covert, secrecy was of the utmost importance, and the subject was not up for discussion. Babe quickly changed the subject. "How long have you been working at the hotel?"

The distraction worked, and like a shiny object or squirrel, Chance went on a tangent about the hotel's history and how he and his family started working with their dad one by one—except Trinity. His opinion was that his sister had a form of ADD and couldn't sit in an office. *Possible*, Babe thought. "Dad said she should run tours, being such a people person. *Interesting thought.*

They stayed at her parents' house for the rest of the afternoon. Learning more about her family spoke to her personality. Despite Antoine Sr.'s edgy business practices, he was a good man and undoubtedly loved his family. Babe watched them as they interacted, which made his mind wander. How would it be with Mays?

Given Babe's unnatural upbringing, he couldn't fathom some warm brotherly reunion. Did Mays have a clue about him? What could he possibly have remembered of his birth parents or childhood? Like his, it had to have been a nightmare the psyche fought to block from memories, yet there would always be an underlying current of darkness. *Thanks, Gino.* Maybe Mays's adoption at five was early enough to paint his childhood with memories of a loving family filled with happiness.

The bottom line was that he'd have to soften some of the rough edges for their child to have a somewhat typical kid life. Was it a possibility? Should he do the child a favor and ghost Trinity? *Food for thought.*

After fond farewells and hugs from Mama Noelle, the boys loaded into the car, full of excitement with stories to tell. In one afternoon, they became a part of a glorious, huge family. All three boys blended in well. No doubt, things might change for poor Jacob once Mama and Papa Noelle learned his story. Maybe, like Ruthie, they would be determined to erase that part of his life and help him overcome the horror.

On the way home, the boys were chatterboxes. Trinity regaled every minute detail about the wedding. The boys listened attentively, as did Babe. Even though it would be a backyard service, he felt sure from the description there would be more pomp and circumstance than he desired.

Once home and settled, the boys hit the sack, and they retired to their room for the night. "Vic, you've been quiet as a church mouse the whole way home. I noticed you with my brothers and Glenn, but you seemed exceptionally quiet even then. You, okay?"

He threw a half-smile. "As I told you in the beginning, I don't talk much. If that's a problem, you need to rethink getting married. Trinity, I've come uncomfortably out of my shell, but I'll never be a Chance or Louis; they could talk to the lamppost." Tears filled her eyes as she climbed into bed, turning her back to him. He pulled change, keys, and a wad of ones out of his pockets, then slipped his pants down. "Am I okay, you asked; the question is, are you okay? What's wrong? Did I say or do something wrong?"

She rolled over, tears running across her face into the pillow. "Do you not want to get married?" She was hurt and angry. "If that's the case, we might as well call it a day and head our separate ways."

He sat hard on the bed, popping her up slightly. "Fuck, no, that's not what I said. I want to make sure you want me for me and not someone you think you can change me into. I am damaged goods, but you know that. Now is your chance to bail if you want." She started sobbing. He moved to her side of the bed and held her. His heart dropped to his stomach. "Trinity, I love you, and I love our alien baby. I start thinking about me, the kind of man I am, and wonder, what kind of father will I be?" She snuggled close to him.

"What kind of parent will either of us be?" She glanced into his eyes. "I'm a bartender, hustling mixed drinks and suggestive dancing for tips. I don't know if I'll be okay with staying at home as a mom. I don't think it's in my makeup. So, you worry about your demons," she held her fingers up with air quotes on demons, "and motherfucking kind of language. See, neither of us knows. This, Babe, is where God and faith come into the picture. Fake it to you make it, my man. God changes lives every second of every day."

He pulled her top over her head, placed her in front of him, and, piece by piece, removed her clothes, then stood and removed his boxer briefs, dropping them on top of his jeans and Trinity's clothes. She tearfully grinned at him as he boldly stated, "If I can leave those there all night, I can change anything. Lay with me. We have to get the kids up in the morning, cook breakfast, and get them on the bus. I'll need my workout, so you'll need to fill in the gaps. Your job is making an appointment with Mays, arranging flights, and booking hotel reservations. My credit card is in my wallet in my jeans in that heap on the floor." He turned off the light, kissed her, and fell asleep with her cuddled against his body.

PHASE THREE: GO

For the most part, the older he got, the faster the days went by, and he found himself waking up Friday morning with a feeling he hadn't felt before. It wasn't butterflies or gas, but almost a vibration coursing his body. All neurons were blasting through the synapses of his being. The morning run turned into five miles of sprinting. Sweat poured off him in buckets, or so it felt. Work whistled by, and it was time to pick up the ring. Off he went to Royal Street.

An exuberant voice from the back rang through the small jewelry store. "Hello, Mr. Vicarelli, I'll be with you in one moment." Babe looked through the glass cases as he waited. Dread filled his mind; what if the rings weren't ready? All the possibilities battered him like a machine gun. Five minutes felt like an hour. *I'm pacing again; what the hell is this about? Pacing, hmm.*

A loud, tornadic flush of the toilet almost shook the glass cases. "Ever since they fixed the commode, one needs to stand away from the powerful whirlpool and not let their dinkler dangle. What a shock that would be. I knew you'd come the minute I went into the toilet. It's the way, but I left the door unlocked for you; usually, I lock it when indisposed." Old people liked to share their toilet habits with anyone who would listen. He remembered his grandfather announcing he had to take his morning constitution. *Shoot me if I get like that,* he thought. "I've been itching to show the beauties to you. Just one more thing, and I can do it in a jiff. What do you want engraved on the inside of her wedding band? I already put the date, since you told me. Some people only want their initials, while others get sappy or, should I say, sentimental.

"Our initials will do. B.R.V. to T.M.N."

"Script or print. The script is always more delicate, although harder to read, but who's reading it? What's your lovely's name, may I ask? Follow me." He led Babe into his work area. The old guy hummed as he began, but it sounded more like staggered grunts.

"Trinity Marie Noelle." He still hadn't seen the ring and was on edge with anticipation. Unconsciously, he began to pace. *What is this fucking pacing about? Composure is key.*

In a sudden and unexpected movement, the jeweler turned around. His eyebrows arched into the same peaks as before. "Antoine's youngest? She's a pepper. Her father and I go way back. In fact, I made Antoinette's engagement ring. Like clockwork, I know I will see my old friend Antoine on every occasion. Of course, he was a mere boy when I designed her engagement ring." Turning back around, he finished engraving. Babe reflected, *Antoine and Antoinette, interesting.* "Prepare yourself, Sonny; the sparkles will blind you." He handed the set over with pride. The engagement ring was impressive; the wedding band had a perfect look with diamonds across the top.

"Beautiful. Thank you." Babe handed over the cash.

Taking two thousand from the stack of money, he handed it back. "Friends and family discount." The man smiled.

"No, sir. That is a kind gesture, but I will pay our agreed-upon price, not a penny less." Babe was determined.

Placing his hands on the case, he commented, obviously amused, "Mr. Vicarelli, you are too sizeable for me to argue. One piece of advice: enjoy your wedding; it's a once-in-a-lifetime occasion, especially in the Noelle family."

Time was ticking. He needed to get home, shower, and dress for the rehearsal. By the time he made it home, Trinity and the boys were dressed and waiting. She was anxious, and according to the boys' comments, she had been looking out the window every few moments. Within fifteen minutes, he was downstairs and ready to go. Her suitcase was by the door. "What's this for?"

Trinity looked at him like he had three heads. "Uh, I can't see you until the wedding. After dinner, you and the boys need to come home. Otherwise, it's bad luck; this girl's not taking any chances."

Babe was surprised but delighted that the boys would be at the rehearsal. Personally, he thought rehearsing for such a small event was over the top, but whatever. If Trinity was happy, that was all that mattered.

The setup at her parents' house was shocking. Mama Noelle, the name she asked people close to the family to call her, had a large tent in her yard, complete with flooring. White wooden chairs, set in rows, flanked the sides, creating a center aisle. The setup crew placed an altar at the end of the aisle, and a piano was up front in a side corner. What the Noelles had put in play was far greater than anything he expected. At a glance, he surmised sixty chairs. *What happened to the priest, Bethany, Glenn, Trinity, and me?* If this was small, he couldn't fathom what Bethany and Glenn's wedding would encompass. Some of the family had already made it there, and more to come.

Babe gladly accepted an offered drink. Antoinette hugged him exuberantly with questions. Who from his family would be in attendance? He thought he'd already explained since the passing of his grandfather, he had no family. They had all died; however, Ruthie and her son would be in attendance. She hugged him again, saying he was now part of a big family. There was no point in going into the possibility of a brother; it'd be like putting the cart before the horse.

Holding up her wine glass, Mama Noelle tapped the side with a spoon to get everyone's attention. Father O'Shea had arrived, and thus, the rehearsal would commence. There was a lot more hoopla than he expected.

Instructions were to stand here, walk there, and say this. Between Trinity's mother and the priest, every t was crossed, and i dotted.

The rehearsal took nearly an hour; then, everyone moved into the house for dinner. Unlike relaxed serve-yourself Sunday dinners, the wait staff had the dining table set for a formal affair. In the adjacent foyer, Mama Noelle had two children's tables set. There was an unobstructed view of the kids from her place at the table. *Good move, Antoinette.* Babe knew the house was big, but it seemed even grander than he remembered. Most of his visits to the house were in the backyard, except for the trip to her bedroom and an improper incident in the bathroom after she cut his hair. He felt a warm flush rising up his neck, recalling how uncomfortable he had felt once he found out Bethany and Glenn lived next door. He wasn't sure he'd like them living next door to his in-laws.

Dinner was a feast with many toasts, tears, and thankfulness. Babe toasted her parents for their hospitality and friendship, then hoisted his glass high and gave a glowing toast to Trinity, saying he knew the first time he saw her at Louie's his heart belonged to her. The night's oddities didn't set off his demons, which was surprising, but the night was still young.

At eleven, Mama Noelle reminded Trinity that Babe needed to gather the boys and head out. It would be bad luck for him to see her beyond midnight. The following day was the wedding, complete with Mass, reception, and then home to finish packing for a week and their flight to Atlanta. Nobody asked where they were going on the honeymoon, but a reference by Trinity included the real honeymoon awaited the arrival of their passports. The extravagant trip was to Norway, where she'd meet Babe's great-uncle, Bjorn. Rolling through his mind was the potential for Mays and his wife to travel with them. *Dreams, Vicarelli creating vulnerability.*

Trinity had scheduled an appointment with Mays for Monday morning, and either they'd be on a plane headed back to New Orleans, or it would go better than expected. The unanswerable questions mounted; perhaps he could fill in the blanks come Monday.

Time ticked on, and while he wasn't bordering on verbose as everyone else, he spoke more than ever. People always questioned about special ops, what Afghanistan was like, and whether he saw much combat. No one ever asked about Africa, South America, Iraq, or any of the other shitholes of service. Babe would teach the boys those were questions never to ask a veteran. Merely thank them for their service and call it a day. No matter how detailed a description one might give, there were no words to lend reality or punctuation to the nightmares. Those memories lived in a hell all their own.

Well-wishes, pats on the back and an occasional hug served to initiate their departure. Trinity walked him to the car. "You gonna show tomorrow, right? Boy, you better not leave me standing at the altar." He sat her on the hood of the car, held her face in his hands, and kissed her sweetly, promising to be there and on time.

"See, Chris," Reg poked him, "that's a sexy kiss, not choking your girl with your tongue down her throat."

"You ever kissed a girl?" Chris asked Reg,

Jacob interrupted, "I have, not just a girl; she was twenty."

Chris scoffed, "Have not."

Jacob became quiet and mumbled, "Have." An immediate hush enveloped the car. They realized they had gone down a path off-limits. Babe opened the door and slid in.

The silence was palpable. Babe gave it a minute to see if anyone would let the cat out of the bag before he inquired. Jacob started to cry.

The tone of Chris's voice indicated his sorrowful feelings. "Jake, I'm sorry, dude. None of that was your fault."

The comment opened the door for the spokesperson, Reg, to tell all. "Sir, that was a nice kiss you gave your lady. I'm sorry I watched, but it was the bomb. I started the whole mess in the car by ragging on Chris. It brought up bad thoughts for Jake, and I'm sorry." Babe gave it some thought.

"Love and sex are two different things. Casual sex and abuse are nothing alike; one's a crime, and the other is getting your jollies. Don't you guys laugh, but I hadn't had a real kiss until Trinity. So, whatever you little dudes got going on is only practice for delivering a dope kiss. No matter who or what, always show respect."

Jacob's crying lightened to slight whimpers. "Sir, if you don't mind me asking. So, if your first kiss was Miss Trinity, when did you lose your virginity?"

Hmm. Truth? Always. "Fourteen, but remember, I was a big kid and looked more like seventeen or eighteen." He glanced in the rearview mirror.

Chris jumped in, "Okay, so let me get this straight. You didn't kiss the girl, but f-had sex? I don't get it. The girls I've been with, you have to kiss them for a month at least before doing anything else and like months for the home run unless they were skanky nasty sluts, and who would want to do them?"

"Since we're being honest here, I'll answer. It was with a working girl. She wasn't much older than me, maybe sixteen, but with the pros, you don't kiss, at least I never did. Trinity was and is my first girlfriend."

Chimes of "No way!" rang through the car. Jacob spoke, "So, you only did it with whores?"

Babe corrected, "Working girls. We don't know why people do what they do. Maybe they are trying to support a child, pay the rent, or attend college. There's a ton of different reasons. Because of the difficult situations, some can only do their job being high on drugs. They feel bad about themselves." As he pulled into the driveway and parked, he asked, "Is it sufficient to say we all understand the respect rule?"

"Yes, sir," and they got out of the car.

Without instruction, they all went to bed.

Morning came faster than usual; the boys were energized with thoughts of the wedding. Ruthie was already back at the house fixing breakfast, and Babe was in the middle of his workout.

Jacob sat on the steps, watching him. "Something on your mind, Jacob?"

Babe could tell the boy was puzzling over the questions as his head waggled from side to side. "Thanks for saying what you did about respect and working girls. I don't know my mother's whole story, only what the—"

"Girls?" the big guy interrupted.

"Yes, only what the girls told me. Maybe that's why she did drugs; she didn't like what she was doing, ya know? They were good to me. I mostly had food and hugs. When I got scared because a pimp or crazy john broke in, they'd let me sleep with them. When I grow up, I'll be happy to give them the money and not expect any sex." He played with a stick on the stairs, chasing an ant. Cocking his head toward his shoulder, "You're a really good guy. I know you don't think you are. I sometimes hear you at night. What you had to do was hard, but you did it. What I had to do to stay alive was hard, but I did it. I'm not embarrassed talking to you, but I don't wanna talk to no one else."

After the workout, he was ready for a run. On a few occasions, one of the boys would want to join him; this morning, he didn't want company, and it was just as well Jacob didn't ask to go.

It was a good run; the time running, losing his thoughts into the breeze, sluffed off any feelings of ambiguity. It was going to be a good day. The shower beckoned, and he took it slow and easy, then laid in bed with the worn Bible. He spent time reading proverbs. "Repent at my rebuke!" he read aloud. "Then I will pour out my thoughts to you, I will make known to you my teachings." (Proverbs 1:23 NIV)

Silently, he spoke to Trinity and Trey's God, begging to be a better man. He asked Him to show the way. Thoughts rambled for an hour; then, he prepared to dress. It had been some time since he'd donned the dress blues. He was particular, making sure everything was square, perfect, Marine proud. His shoes were reflective as a mirror, sheer perfection. Babe had worn his uniform proudly and, seeing himself in the mirror, tugged at his heart, filling it with the embodiment of a Marine he held so dear.

As he descended the stairs, Reg was on the way up the stairs. "Holy Shit, y'all come see, come see." The boys and Ruthie rushed over, and a hush came over them. A lump developed in his throat; Babe pressed his tongue to the roof of his mouth, forcing the wannabe tears to subside.

"Lordy, Lordy. You make a fine picture, Marine. You do that uniform proud. Has your girl ever seen you in it?" He answered, no, ma'am. "She's like to fall out." Ruthie squinted, wrinkling the corners of her eyes, pursing her lips. "Yes, indeed, Miss Trinity Noelle's heart is gonna be all in a flutter." Babe checked his pockets for the rings; his cell phone was in his pocket, already on silent. He grabbed a glass for a two-finger pour.

On the drive over to the Noelle's, he called Glenn. The one thing he didn't know was where he needed to wait out of sight. "Your timing is perfect. Park in front of our house so you're not fighting to get your car out when you leave. The girls and Mama Noelle are taking pictures. You coming from the Quarter?" He replied no, uptown. "I'll meet you outside my house, and we can walk over together. Make sure to give me the ring."

With time to spare, he waited at the front door. Glenn yelled for him to come in; he'd left the door unlocked. Babe opened the door. He stood waiting in the foyer. When Glenn saw him, his mouth went agape. "Holy shit, brotha, you look amazing. Fuck, she's gonna flip. You look like the fucking poster for the Marines. I gotta say, it suits you. I know Antoine wouldn't want to hear me say it, but I could so see you rejoining or whatever it's called. But, don't, ya hear."

Glenn was still sputtering about his presence in the uniform on the walk next door. When they entered the tent, Babe stopped him, handed the rings over, and thanked him. They both chuckled at how tiny the rings were but beautiful. "So her parents will approve of these?"

"Uh, yeah. You set the bar way high. Fortunately, Bethany only wanted a solitaire, nothing as spectacular as that," holding the rings to the light.

They walked to the end of the aisle where the altar was, then over to the side like Antoinette had instructed. The massive floral arrangements provided a barrier of sorts, but they could be seen by those sitting in the second and third rows.

The tent began filling up; Babe watched for Coach. The time was drawing near; the pianist started playing background music. People began clambering for a seat, everyone wanting a seat on the aisle. Ruthie, Clive, and the boys entered. Two of Trinity's brothers escorted them to the front row on the right. The boys whispered, pointing at Babe. Ruthie leaned forward, gave them a look, and the shenanigans stopped promptly. Shep entered dressed in a dark suit, starched shirt, and pink tie. His wife, an attractive bosomy brunette probably a decade his junior, wore a black dress with pink buttons down the front. They coordinated; he knew Trinity would appreciate that look. Finn and his date arrived. She was a cute girl with bouncy, dirty blonde curls. The similarities to Jessica Lambert, the girl who died on Spring Break, were uncanny. Finn sat on the right, meaning eight guests on his side. It caused a chuckle. He wondered if Samantha was on the guest list. Jack Kennedy entered; he was Marine proud in dress blues. He and his wife, a sassy-looking redhead, sat on the right. Jack winked at Babe. Dr. Landry and his wife Rainie entered with their five children and sat in the fourth row on his side. Was that by instruction from Mama Noelle, or had Rainie made the decision?

Once the seats filled, the pianist stopped playing momentarily, signaling Glenn and Babe to move to their appointed positions. The crowd reacted to his appearance with startle and admiration. He smiled with a cock-eyed grin. Under his breath, Glenn commented, "You know how to make a statement." Babe realized he had his black rubber wedding band on; he'd forgotten to give it to Trinity. They'd figure it out, *no worries*. He slipped it off his finger and palmed it. Antoinette, escorted by Antoine Jr., entered, smiling at all the guests as she walked down the aisle. Then Bethany, dressed in an Autumn Orange strapless, made her appearance. Her eyes were glossy with tears waiting to fall. Following her was one of the nieces sprinkling flowers along the aisle.

A trumpeter filled the tent with music, announcing the bride. Nothing could have prepared him for the sight of his beloved. The dress was beautiful, an off-white strapless form-fitting her hips and flowing in a mermaid style. The top of the dress had a four-inch forest of shiny copper and orange leaves.

Metallic shimmering leaves cascaded as an expression of autumn, enhancing the embellishmment. It was remarkable. The veil was illusory sheer with an edge to match her dress, giving him a silhouette of her face. Antoine's eyes told a story; he was proud of his new son-in-law. Babe knew he presented well in his dress blues.

The ceremony went without a hitch. When he tried to pass the black silicone ring to her, he saw a slight shake of her head. A soloist sang Ave Maria, bringing on tears from Trinity and building fullness in his chest, another new feeling. The priest put her rings on a pillow, and Bethany handed the priest a ring identical to Trinity's wedding band. The bands were blessed, the vows said, and then the priest said Babe could kiss his bride. His heart doubled-timed thinking about his bride and the wild conversation with the boys. She was beautiful, overwhelming his breath. Ruthie patted her eyes with a handkerchief; Jack even had tears resting on his lids. While it was an entire Mass, the time seemed to slip by like a whimsical dream.

Since they were the first ones out of the tent, they could speak privately, "Vic, wow, you look unbelievable. I didn't know you were wearing your uniform. It looks like you and the rings OMG. They had to be a fortune." She held his hands.

"Speaking of rings, I thought my black silicone band was it. I know where you got it. Mr. Kahn, with a K, could have told me you were getting it. Sneaky old bastard. Did he tell you?" He held her tightly and kissed her. "I'll have to tell you about a conversation with the boys later. You will find it amusing with a particle of sadness." People started filing out of the tent.

"No, Levi didn't say a word, crafty. He's here, ya know?" The well-wishes, hugs, and kisses began.

For someone who didn't like to be touched, he managed with a constant flow of closeness from people he had no idea who they were. Jack was most interested in meeting Trinity. "Ma'am, you and I need to sit and talk sometime. You, pretty lady, are the answer to this coach's prayer. I'll tell you all about ya boy. Helluva a man, you got."

"Yes, I do, sir. He's the best."

MY BRO OR NO

The reception was unlike any party he'd ever been to. Trinity must have clued her mom on the need for slow music when dancing involved him. After a couple of hours, he was ready to be home. The mass of people crowding him had been uncomfortable, and given Trinity's stature, she'd disappear in a circle of guests, another item to add to his list of do-not-likes. Babe realized he was a bit over the top and needed to relax.

He moved through the guests around her and stood by her side. One by one, they fanned off to converse with other family members. "Atlanta tickets done and appointment with Mays confirmed?" The corner of her mouth turned up. He'd been social at the reception, not awkward or scary silent. She could tell when it was time to leave. His eyes darted through the crowd, assuring all was well.

Given the heightened state of Folsom at Inez's farm, he and Big Paul could communicate with each other, and he seemed more comfortable. She noticed the two of them chuckling, if that was what one would call it, both having an almost expressionless face. Trinity noticed that while everyone called the man Big Paul, Babe just called him Paul, which would follow since her man was larger than her dad's bodyguard.

Trinity came up behind them. "Babe, let's say our goodbyes and head to the apartment. We can sleep in or whatever tomorrow since we went to Mass today." The happy couple bid farewell and took off in the truck with a trail of cans strung to his vehicle and writing on the rear window. The world would know they'd just been married so much for anonymity.

His phone dinged with a picture of them leaving her parents. The number wasn't familiar, but he suspected Javier was the author of the text. The next question was who had infiltrated Antoine's inner circle. It was one more thing to add to his list of queries when they came home. Babe needed to pass the message on to Antoine without upsetting him. "You recognize the number?" he asked Trinity. She looked at the phone, quickly jotted it down, and called the number. Going down Marconi with City Park on their left, he made a sharp left, crossing the neutral ground while observing the rearview. No one pursued. Once in the park, he pulled over, jumped out of the car, and removed the strings of cans. He checked everything, no trackers. He swept the truck thoroughly. "All clear."

Trinity leaned out of the window. "What in the hell are you doing? You're scaring me." Nobody answered the call from the mystery number. She texted back, but there was no reply. He slid back into the truck. "Is something wrong?" They drove off, but she watched him constantly looking in his rearview and out the windows. "Hello?"

"I think everything is fine, my girl. So, have you decided to be Trinity Noelle-Vicarelli or leave the Vic completely off and go by your maiden name? Fuck, it opens more doors, that's for damn sure." His eyes twinkled as he looked at her. "Whatever you want. I know I told you how gorgeous you look, but that is an outstanding dress. Your mom created an idyllic setting; everything was surreal. I thought it would be you, me, the priest, your parents, Bethany and Glenn, and, of course, Ruthie and the boys."

Going down Orleans, a black SUV pulled in front of them, and one pulled behind, riding their bumper. "Hang on, girl." He punched the accelerator and swerved into the next lane, racing the engine, making a sharp turn, and squealing into the French Quarter. The black vehicles continued down Rampart and didn't turn into the Quarter—*false alarm.*

They pulled into the parking garage and went to the apartment.

Babe lifted his tiny lady and crossed the threshold. Trinity giggled, "Who would have thought you'd be such a sentimental romantic? Boy, you keep surprising me." On the counter was a basket with wine, champagne, chocolate truffles, and bougie snacks. The card indicated it was Javier. "I know he's all badass cartel, but I think he is your friend. Now, don't get me wrong, please stay well away from Cartagena and him."

Unlike usual, the cleaning service made the bed and freshened her room. It smelled like a hotel room and not her beachy diffuser scent. Babe carefully loosened the ties up the back of her dress, and it fell to the floor. She had on matching undergarments complete with nylons and a garter belt. "Not like you. Even with that tiny baby bump, you are the sexiest woman alive." Keeping his eyes trained on her, Babe took off his uniform, carefully hanging it, ready to be brought home and safely tucked away in a garment bag.

"You in your uniform sent a heat wave through my body. I am in dire need of you." He crouched by the side of the bed, removing her shoes and delicately relieving her of her beautiful but scandalous undergarments. "Believe it or not, the lingerie was a gift from my mom. I kinda blushed when I unwrapped the present. I don't want my mother to think of me in your clutches, but speaking of—"

Babe pulled her to him for a most blissful wedding night.

"Trinity, you need to get a move on. We need to be at the airport in two hours. C'mon, girl, get the lead out." How could she tell him about being afraid to fly? The man had flown in every kind of aircraft and parachuted into enemy territory; nonetheless, she was nervous. Carrying all three suitcases, he ushered her out of the door. "What's up? Nervous about meeting Mays? You're gonna breeze right through it. Maybe he'll tell me to get the fuck out or not remember anything from childhood. I'm the one being tongue-tied. Don't you worry, my girl."

"It's not that Vic. I'm nervous about f—"

He looked sideways at her, "Flying? If so, know many of the passengers on our flight will be nervous, so you're not alone. I can sorta understand; the first time I jumped, I was trepidatious, we all were. Our instructor reminded us that everyone has their day to die, so there was no point in worrying about it. The day would come for us all. While it may sound morbid, it spoke volumes to me; therefore, not much shakes me unless it involves you." He smiled and winked at her. "I got ya back; have no fear. Hold my hand and squeeze tight if you need to."

The tremble inside her body slowly left. Everything he had said was true. Her mama had said countless times, 'No one is guaranteed tomorrow.' Babe loaded all the bags onto the airport shuttle. The driver was a chatty woman, asking all the usual travel questions. What did they think of New Orleans? How long had they visited? Babe politely cut her off, saying they were locals. With a one-eighty-degree turn, the questions began as to their destination. *Woman, please, shut the fuck up.* All the chatter started winding Trinity up rather than creating a distraction. He held her hand with a soft squeeze.

Once out of the Quarter, the shuttle headed at a good clip toward the airport. Since no other passengers were onboard, they whispered back and forth about Mays and her planned approach. Babe made sure the transition into the airport went smoothly, trying to keep her mind on positive things. They talked about the wedding and the guests. It was simple.

Her body stiffened as they entered the aircraft. They were in seats 2A and B. "Girl, are you crazy? First-class? This is a first for me."

"Oh, excuse me, I think private jet rates higher than first class. I figured I'd make the best out of a scary situation, but my fear factor has decreased. Ask me why." She poked him in the ribs and then explained that when doing a speech or presentation in school, they said to picture everyone in their underwear, but now she took it a step further and imagined him naked and ready.

The flight attendant, checking their seat belts and trays, looked at her with a quizzical expression, head stiffly tilted and eyebrows raised. Babe found it amusing, considering Trinity blushed three shades of red, which glowed through her velvety caramel skin.

Minutes later, they were speeding down the runway. He could tell she was beginning to get nervous again, inspiring him to tell the story about the boys and firsts. "I never told you about the conversation with the kids. Get a load of this—evidently, when we kissed good night after the rehearsal dinner, Reg tells Chris that our kiss was sexy or how it should be. The subject expands to sex, first-time experience, you know, the bragging bullshit kinda stuff. Jacob blurted out that his first kiss was with a twenty-year-old; Chris argued with the 'yeah, right,' but things went silent, and Jacob began to cry. I got in the car, asked what was wrong, and then the questions directed at me, still first-time, etcetera." She had bought into the conversation, changing focus from fear of the flight to hanging onto his every word.

Trinity's forehead lightly creased. "Jacob is twelve. Sex with a twenty-year-old?" She became quiet and thoughtful. "I never thought about what those kids go through. I bet they subjected the poor little guy to all kinds of perversity."

Babe rested her head against his chest, tenderly stroking her hair. "You have no idea; it's horrendous. One day, when we haven't anything pressing, I'll give you some broad strokes, but we need to review the Mays plan." His mind flashed his internal debate regarding the three thugs who robbed and shot innocents. To plan or let things happen organically? In the moment, spontaneous measures worked best for him. Maybe they should wing it and see how it played out.

The aircraft ran into insignificant turbulence, and Trinity held tight to him. Babe gave it his best shot at explaining aerodynamics and why there was nothing to fear. *Effort failed;* she clutched even tighter. "Think of it like driving on a street with a few potholes. They jar but don't do anything except maybe spill your coffee." He kissed the top of her head. In so many ways, she had the innocence of a young girl; in other ways, she was almost more woman than he could handle. His pulse soared with thoughts of her and how she had calmed the beast inside while awakening his soul. She ignited him; they could kindle the fire once alone at the hotel.

"I wish I could drink; perhaps if I had a buzz going, I wouldn't be such a nervous nelly. You've done an excellent job of allaying my fear. We used to fly everywhere as a family. My dad brought us to Paris, London, Montreal, and New York, all over God's creation. As a kid, I was never scared. The vacations were exciting; I always loved to travel. I guess I was young and never gave it a second thought; it was an adventure." The captain came over the PA, announcing their descent, weather conditions, and temperatures. He sounded friendly, and other than the few small segments of turbulence, the flight was smooth.

Baggage claim was a breeze; she'd heard so many luggage nightmares but knew her man would handle whatever needed his attention. She watched women and men do a double, often triple, take of her built husband. His body was insane, and all hers. He didn't take notice or was numb to the attention but scanned the airport, his eyes missing nothing.

Trinity had booked their accommodation at the Intercontinental Buckhead Atlanta. Mays' firm was in close proximity, making it easy for them to get to their morning appointment. Arriving before check-in, they left their bags at the front desk and went sightseeing. Being so accustomed to a barrage of travelers, Trinity felt giddy being a tourist. She and Babe took selfies at every stop, laughing and cutting up like a young couple in love.

Four o'clock finally rolled around, and both were eager to get into their hotel room. Finally, alone, they spent the afternoon and evening in each other's arms. His woman was as primal as he was at the very core.

Their sexploits were followed by a shower and an eight o'clock dinner, returning to the room for plenty of sleep and the excitement of meeting Mays in the morning.

Wind whipping between buildings gave her a slight shiver. It was much cooler than New Orleans. Her hair flurried around her face, catching in her eyelashes and mouth. Once inside the office building, Trinity primped, looking at her reflection in the glass door. She tugged on his shirt, "I look okay?"

"Way better than okay, my girl. It's hard keeping my hands off you." He appeared calm without the slightest indication of apprehension. Trinity marveled at his composure. He was a man in control.

The elevator arrived at the third floor. Before them were two oversized wooden doors with the firm's name in gold-tone metal lettering. He opened the door for her. Welcoming them was a young lady, perhaps Trinity's age, with a toothpaste commercial smile. "Can I help you?"

Trinity squared her shoulders, answering, "Trinity Noelle, to see Mays Connolly. We have a nine o'clock meeting. Clutching her shoulder bag close to her body, she followed the woman with Babe closely behind. She turned at a corner office. "This way." There was a sizeable man on the telephone. He was every bit as tall as Babe, obviously big-boned, but more fat on the bones than he probably wanted. He ended the call, and as he turned, he said, "so sorry." His round blue eyes jetted to Babe. "I'll be damned. I know you, sir. The hows and whys are a long story. Please take a seat. His smile was warm and noticeably sharper on one side. His eyes volleyed between Trinity and Babe.

Trinity looked down at her hands. "It's Trinity Vicarelli." The man's eyes popped wide. "I'm afraid I may have come here on false pretenses, but you seem to have twigged onto the situation faster than I thought possible."

Babe and Mays locked eyes. "You look like him, but I guess you know that. I often wondered if they would have another child. I hoped not for the child's sake, but here you are." When either Trinity or Babe would speak, Mays would turn his head to the right and lean into their voice, watching their lips. "If you had light hair, you'd look exactly like—"

"Farfar? Yes, he passed this year. He was a handful and the most important person in my life until—" He nodded toward Trinity. "I spent most of my time at their house. Our mother wasn't well, and the sperm donor wasn't the sort to be around." The conversation broadened as the brothers spoke of their parents, the horrid situation, and Babe's twelve-year-old actions of maiming Gino.

Mays interrupted, "So, your name?"

A big smile crossed his face, "Babe. You know who named you?" They both laughed.

"Please speak a little louder; I'm deaf in my left ear and have hearing loss in my right." She saw the redness climb Babe's neck. He asked if the hearing issues had anything to do with Gino. Mays nodded but said he didn't remember much but never forgot their grandfather and always wondered as a kid why they put him up for adoption. "I understood as an adult, the psycho would have always been a part of my life. Shit, I can't believe it's you. How'd you find out about me?" Mays put his hand up and buzzed his secretary, asking her to cancel all the appointments for the day except his ten thirty; it wasn't enough notice. "How long are you going to be in town?"

Trinity explained they had come specifically to meet him and planned to spend whatever it took for them to reconnect. "I can't believe you recognized Babe."

"He looks identical to our grandfather except for the dark hair, but he got that from our father." The conversation moved to Babe's law school and decision to join the Marines. "You certainly look the part. After my ten thirty, which shouldn't be more than an hour, I'd love to take you to meet my wife, Lissa. The kids are in school, with three boys and one spoiled girl, William, in honor of our grandfather, who named me after Willie Mays. I know the man's name was Willie, but I couldn't do that to the boy, so I made it more formal, thus William. Then we have Princess Paige, Maddox, and Tanner. So, how'd you find out, never mind gives us much to talk about at lunch and dinner. Where do you live?"

Trinity explained who she was and said that they now live uptown.

She talked a lot about herself and then released the bomb about a baby on the way. Mays' face lit up. They spoke about current issues and laughed more about Rune, their grandfather. Her heart filled with stacked-up tears. The whole brother reunion was part of God's plan, and it was good. Mays' ten-thirty appointment arrived. He escorted them to a conference room, instructing his secretary to get them whatever they wanted, and he left, promising not to be too long with his appointment.

"So, my big man, thoughts?" She sipped on a glass of water.

He relaxed back in the chair. "Fuck, he looks exactly like my mother. I was shocked that he recognized me as family. He was only five years old when he was adopted. I'm amazed he remembers so much. I will ask him if he wants to share in our grandfather's estate, and I'll be happy to do so. I want to know if he has anger issues or if his kids rage. Did you notice we have similar smiles?" Trinity listened to him babble on. Babe had never been very chatty, and all of a sudden, he wouldn't stop talking. Yes, he started speaking more as their relationship developed, but this was like turning on a spigot, maybe closer to opening a fire hydrant. Babe had a lifetime of things to share and learn about his brother. She wondered if they'd all travel to Norway together. Having a sibling one didn't know was a foreign concept to her. It'd be like her dad or mom having a child she hadn't met. The Noelles were a tight bunch and had always been.

Mays came out of the meeting and joined them in the conference room, grabbing his valise and meandering the hall to the reception area. "We're heading out. I'll be gone most of the week. Bridget," he turned, laying a hand on the younger's shoulder, "This is my brother Babe and his wife, Trinity." She could see both men's chests swell and their breath hitch. If she could have recorded the moment, she would have. Her big guy belonged as a Marine to something much bigger than himself but never had a sense of being a part of anything else except her. She was a Noelle through and through, always had been and always would be, and now he had a brother that he could share in a united front. Trinity had to fight back the tears. She had the same feeling as from a drippy love story made for Hallmark.

While Mays was obviously older and a bit heftier, the two had the same swagger to their walk, perfect posture, and similar gestures. Even though their coloring was different, there was no doubt they were brothers. A block down, Mays turned into a parking garage. Babe carefully listened to every word his older brother had to say. Taillights flickered, unlocking the doors to a Range Rover SV. It was a big vehicle, a bit like Babe's truck. The car was beautiful, and she suspected at least two hundred thousand. *Okay, he's a successful attorney, got it.* Mays spoke most of the ride about Buckhead and how great a place it was to raise kids. He had two in high school, one in eighth and one in seventh. They went to Christ The King School, and the older ones went to Atlanta International School. She gathered the school was prestigious. He was as chatty as she, barely taking a breath. Not that anyone inquired, but he explained the younger children would attend AIS after graduating from Christ The King. Lissa was adamant about Catholic education. *Yay, his brother is a believer,* she thought.

Sitting at a red light, the older reached over, squeezing Babe's shoulder. "You're built like a brick shithouse. You work out every day, I bet." Babe nodded. "I used to be built, not as big as you, but well-built in college until Lissa became pregnant with William." She leaned forward and patted Babe on the shoulder, clearing her throat.

"Trinity has told me all," emphasizing 'all,' "about men experiencing weight gain during their wives' pregnancies. I'm going to be on high alert. I have to keep my strength and skills for my calling per se." His arms rested on his thighs. Trinity bragged about the rescue mission. "I don't want to inundate you with my trivia. We have a few days to touch on everything, but I have things to ask later if you don't mind."

Mays asked all the questions one might consider, and like everyone, the first was why he became a Marine after completing law school and passing the bar. Babe found it curious; only another Marine could understand the calling.

The car pulled up to a beautiful, massive home. One of the bays of his four-car garage opened. "Sorry to take you in through the garage. I'm sure Lissa will have a fit."

An elegant Asian woman came from the door with her hands turned upward and brows lifted. "Really, Mays!" She looked at Babe and Trinity. "Hi, I'm Lissa. Sorry, my husband is bringing you through the garage. Please come in." She kissed her husband as he walked by.

He led the way into a den off of the kitchen, telling everyone to take a seat. "Lis, I thought we could go to lunch; however, I have an interesting story to regale before we go." He pointed at the couple. "Honey, this is my brother Babe and his wife Trinity." His eyes got misty. "They found me and came to the office today. He looks exactly like the Viking, only dark hair." He looked at Babe, "That's what I call him, The Viking. He looked like a Viking, don't you think?" Babe read the wife, and she was skeptical, waiting for the catch or scam. *Sorry, lady, this is no hustle.*

"On that note, sweetheart, I think we can open a bottle of wine and celebrate." Trinity offered to help, remarking water would be better, at least for her. "Please relax. I'll bring you some water." She walked out of the room. Mays sat in a wingback recliner chair, pointing to the sofa. Mays was as warm and welcoming as possible, but Lissa was a fire-breathing bitch with suspicions. She came back in with three wine glasses and a glass of water. "Where are you from? And what brings you to Buckhead?" She sat perched on the edge of her seat with an unnatural stiffness.

Babe and Trinity answered simultaneously, "New Orleans. To meet Mays." One brow went up. Babe began, "Lissa, it's quite a story, fair warning. After our grandfather died, he left everything to me. I am a simple man and don't have many needs. He had one remaining brother, Bjorn, in Norway. I called him to see if he wanted any of the old guy's things. Bjorn is quite a character and was somewhat intoxicated when I called. He didn't want anything, and I asked if there were any other family members. He let it slip about Mays and the situation. Finding out I had a brother was shocking, and I wanted to meet him." He looked at Mays. "I wanted to see if you'd like any of Far's things or half the inheritance; it's sizeable. I see you do well," he waved his hand around the room. "But, whatever you want." He turned his head back toward Lissa, "So after much research, we found him. Because he looked so much like my mother, I knew it had to be him, also the name. Our grandfather had a thing for baseball, hence, Mays as in Willie Mays, and Babe as in Babe Ruth. We decided that instead of taking an average honeymoon, we'd find my brother. Trinity and I were married on Saturday. I didn't know if he would find any similarities or remember anything since he was so young, but he did right away."

She sat spellbound. Looking between Trinity and Babe, she said, "Certainly, you can understand my curiosity," turning her palm up and sweeping her hand slightly. "I'm afraid my husband is quite gullible, whereas I am far more discerning. Tell me a little about yourself." Babe unpacked the story, including the part where he maimed his father at twelve. The woman gasped, and Mays congratulated him. Once again, when he got to the law school part, she didn't get the Marine decision.

Trinity had her hand on Babe's thigh and felt the muscles contract. She glanced at his face and noticed the pink rising up his neck. He did not like his brother's wife, not at all. No thank you for your service, which was rude, and her tone seemed demeaning. She loaded both barrels and blasted.

Trinity began her story. His lady could talk and took great offense when someone implied anything but greatness about her man. "I met Babe at one of my family's establishmments. You see," she paused, "I'm a Noelle. My family owns a few hotels in the French Quarter, one of the world-famous bars, and a restaurant. My dad," she flicked both her wrists upward, "has the main restoration and construction company in the Quarter, as well as, several other businesses. I had hoped we could move into my house in Lakeview since Babe rescued three boys from being abducted by the cartel, but," she sighed, "he wanted to raise them in the uptown house. Ruthie, the caretaker at the house, has done a fabulous job with the boys. Of course, Babe pays for all their schooling and is seeing for all their needs—private education and the like." Babe took her hand and squeezed it, saying that was enough. Trinity looked at him with a huge smile. "He is my love, a real-life superhero." Babe almost choked, thinking, *Boy, she must be pissed.* It was the first time he'd seen that side of her, and he had to acknowledge to himself it was impressive.

Mays was sincere in his comments. "God, Babe, rescue missions dealing with a cartel? Since you are no longer in the service, why would you consider doing something so dangerous?" His frowning brows created two vertical lines forming an eleven; his face took on a grimaced look with lips drawn and a sense of worry in his eyes. "Weren't you scared? I mean, cartel. That's heavy-duty shit."

Babe scanned the room, taking it all in. It was no wonder the man didn't get it. Mays' life was completely different than his. Their upbringing was like night and day. His life after five had been soft, cushy, and good for him. He bore no resentment. Although it had taken time, he finally was able to absorb some of the goodness of the world. *Thank you, Trinity.* There were a few family portraits starting when there was one child, then two, three, and four. Yes, Mays was not quite as pudgy when they were babies. The family photos captured the metamorphosis of both Mays and Lissa. The bigger his waist stretched, the thinner she became. He guessed Lissa was about five-four and maybe a buck twenty, probably closer to fifteen. Her silky black hair had a severe look, with a chin-length blunt cut. He couldn't help but notice Mays was easygoing, whereas Lissa seemed more to have a snotty, stick-up-the-ass demeanor.

Trinity had shut down the condescension in Lissa's attitude. They spent the rest of the afternoon at a lengthy lunch. One thing for sure was

Mays liked his food, and Lissa enjoyed her wine. There was an undercurrent of dissatisfaction between the two. They planned the next day's activities. There couldn't have been four more different people. She knew the thing Babe wanted the most was to talk about rage or mental dysfunction.

Two days into their reunion, Babe spoke with Mays about his five years with Gino; it was far more than anticipated. The hearing loss resulted from their father's temper, which roused Babe's inner struggles, creating a conduit for eliminating the wretch. The bastard had gotten away with too much, and the only repercussion ever dealt out was by a twelve-year-old boy who had had enough. Whether it was because Gino's rage lived in him or he always needed to right the wrongs was anyone's guess.

Doctors, counselors, and social workers had converged on a sociopathic, maybe even psychopathic, personality disorder diagnosis. As an adult, he knew he had legal rights to his medical file, yet once retrieved, there wasn't a mention of such a diagnosis. He'd been told too often about it to believe he'd made the whole thing up. Was it a delusion? Who told him about the mental illness? Had he spun the falsehood? When they returned to New Orleans, he would hunt down Gino Vicarelli and get answers one way or another. Sources to open doors might be his military psychiatrist, his mentor, Coach Kennedy, and his pediatrician if he was still alive. He remembered old Dr. Hudson with a head full of silver hair and glasses with coke bottle lenses. As a young boy, the doctor seemed ancient, but as a child, anyone with silver hair was a dinosaur.

Meeting his nephews and niece was almost as overwhelming as reuniting with his brother. Mays' daughter Paige was the image of his mother, beautiful beyond words and with a demeanor equally as lovely. The older son, William, resembled Mays, Maddox, the third child had features like Lissa, and Tanner could have easily been Babe's son. As a seventh grader, he was tall and roped with natural muscle. If the boy decided to weight train, he had no doubt he'd beef up with a similar body type.

While it was a terrific experience and a joy-filled night, Babe was ready to have Trinity alone in their room at the hotel. It was a quick ride. She curled in his arms, snuggling into his body. It appeared their plans had set a course for new relationships and a bold new world for them.

After a healthy breakfast, he and Trinity cabbed it to Mays' home the following morning. Close to the door, they heard Lissa screeching, berating comments toward his brother. Not that it was his business, but it made him wonder if this was what the man put up with on a regular basis. Poor man, Babe was confident he'd had enough criticism and abuse as a youngster. Trinity rang the doorbell; her dander was up. He could see it in her eyes. In two days, his woman had developed a heart-filled fondness for Mays. In her words, he was like a giant teddy bear. The men were as different as night and day, yet somehow seemed the same.

Composed, Lissa greeted them as the perfect hostess. "Mays is still in the shower; he'll be down in a second. Coffee, anyone?"

"No, we had breakfast, thank you," Trinity remarked.

Babe stood with his hands on his hips, wanting desperately to ask her why the abusive behavior toward Mays. *Not my place.* He cracked half a smile. "Looking at your neighborhood, I noticed a sign for a nature hike. Maybe Mays and I could hike for a bit. I can't go days without working out, and I'm afraid the gym at the hotel is not my speed."

Lissa scoffed, "I doubt you could get him to agree. He's lazy. One look at him, and you can tell." Babe put his arm around Trinity's waist with a squeeze, giving the signal, do not interfere. "All he does is work, work, work. I'm surprised he took time off to be with you." She rolled her eyes. Upon hearing the woman, he certainly understood why Mays stayed at the office. To afford her lifestyle probably required hours at the office. The man was worn down. "Take a seat in the living room; he shouldn't be too much longer. I'll go get him."

Trinity chirped in, "Don't bother; we can visit until he's ready. If he's anything like Babe, he loves his shower. It's a time to unwind without me yacking in his ear." The woman grabbed her coffee cup and sat across from them. "So, Lissa, I told you all about me. I'd love to hear your story. Where were you born? You have that silky hair; it's so beautiful. How'd the two of you meet?"

Babe saw the register of discomfort; Lissa had skeletons in her closet. With a limp wrist, she flicked her hand and avoided the question. *Mays' wife or not, my little pit bull isn't letting go without answers, especially after the berating, yelling, and screaming.* He watched her shift uncomfortably in her chair. Sitting with her head held upward, almost as if looking down her nose, she coyly replied, "My family lives in Southeast Asia."

Trinity's eyes rounded wide, "Wow, that must be a long trip to visit them. How long of a flight?"

"It's been a very long time since I've seen them." Cut and dry, no emotion.

Trinity steepled her hands as though praying, "How awful. I'm so sorry." *She's laying it on thick.*

His girl pepped up, "How'd y'all meet? I mean, Asia and Atlanta?" She held her hands like scales, putting them up and down, bouncing her head from side to side. "Were you like in college or—" Trinity had rocked the boat a little too hard. Lissa became edgier. Her lips formed a tight line, almost a grimace.

Just as she was about to answer, Mays came around the corner. "I got the tail end of your conversation. Lissa was the woman for me. I knew it from the pictures of her, so I brought her here, and we got married. It's been sixteen years." *Ah-ha,* Babe thought, *mail-order bride.* They could be brutal, just from the few he'd met. It was as though they had to punish the men who chose them.

Laying it on thick, Trinity cooed, "How sweet, love at first sight. Ya know I knew I wanted Babe the first time I saw him, but, truth be told, it was all lust." She giggled and put her hand to her face as though feigning embarrassment. "He didn't talk at all at first, but I buttered him up. He'd say," she lowered her voice, trying to imitate him, "Ma'am, a two-finger pour of Glenlivet, then I said," she laughed again. "My two fingers or yours? I had to get that ball rolling, or I think he would have sat at my bar for years without saying a word."

Babe scoffed, saying it wasn't quite so dramatic. The atmosphere lightened a little. "Mays, after your coffee, you want to hike with me? I saw where your neighborhood has a nature trail." He was all for it, saying he didn't need the coffee. The fresh air would make an excellent wake-up call."

"I got this, Babe," she whispered in a kiss. "Enjoy your brother."

MORE THAN
A WALK

7he two men walked side by side. "I guess you heard Lissa's temper. She's not always like that." He felt like he had to defend her. *But why?* Babe thought.

"That's between y'all—none of my business. My only comment is you sure as shit don't deserve anyone talking to you poorly. I've been around a few mail-order girls who started out as brides. They resented the," and he used air quotes, "rich American men, but y'all been together sixteen years and have four kids. Has it always been like that?" Silence. Babe stayed quiet as they walked. He stopped Mays, "Shh, look between the trees," he pointed, "There's a doe and her two fawns." They remained quiet and watched for a few minutes, then continued walking.

The crisp air was at least ten degrees cooler than New Orleans. The sky was clear, not a cloud in sight. "In all the years we've lived here, I've never walked the nature trail. Thanks, this is great." They pressed on. "You exercise every day?"

Babe nodded. "Trinity and I are going to Norway as soon as our passports arrive. Y'all oughta come with us. I'm sure you take off work from time to time. Think about it. I want to visit Bjorn, and we have to go before Trinity is too far along." There was a moment of consternation. Babe could almost palpate Mays's thoughtful energy. "While you ponder that, I have a question. Do you or any of your kids have a dark side, like rage? I do, and it scares the shit out of me that our baby might have the darkness." Mays commented that he had the opposite problem. "You're not weak, you know. It takes far more strength to keep your cool than react. Don't beat yourself up—"

Mays interrupted with tears cascading down his cheeks. "No, I'm weak, afraid to say. I want to curl in a ball and disappear." He put his hand on Babe's shoulder.

They kept walking. "How badass are you in the courtroom? From what I've read, you are one savvy motherfucker. You've won some impressive cases." Babe winked at him. "I did my research. My problem is," he hesitated. "I wasn't a violent person until Gino pushed one too many times, but once I settled it, the anger was gone. I had kids pick on me sometimes in school, and I coulda beat the living crap out of them, but I didn't. I restrained them and usually got sent to the office because they always thought because I was bigger, I must have been the culprit. One day, Coach Kennedy saw some kids harassing me. I coulda done major damage to the little pricks but didn't, and they ended up in the office for once instead of me. Coach was a Marine, and I respected him. The Corps taught and molded me. I can be one mean motherfucker, but I'm reasonable. People want to pick fights with me more times than you can imagine, and I always say, 'Don't pick a fight you can't win.' I have skills and can teach you, my brother. It's empowering whether you use it or not; you know it's at your disposal. Understand? I take it too far on occasion because someone pisses me off by hurting an innocent. Oh, and I'm sure you'll hear this or may even see it; the psychiatric community postulates that I have PTSD, although never a written diagnosis. I have illusory visions from the past."

He could see Mays was chewing on what he'd said. Babe picked up the pace, and his brother matched him. "Yeah, I might want to go to Norway. If Lissa won't go, will I be a third wheel with you and Trinity?"

"Are you kidding me? Hell, no. I hope you join us." He started a slow jog.

"Are you trying to kill me?" He joined in the jog. "You know CPR?"

Babe laughed after Mays' question. As they neared the end, he grabbed Babe's arm, "We can do this tomorrow?"

"And more."

"I have a steam and sauna at the house, a pool and spa as well. I want to talk more. You asked about a short fuse temper; William has a short fuse, but the others don't. I get angry and cry. I know you think I'm a pussy."

Babe turned around and faced him with a serious, determined look. "No, I don't. You're a big man, and I bet you'd scare yourself if you reacted with anger. It would remind you of—"

"Maybe." Mays nodded at the possibility.

Babe started heading toward the house, "Put a heavy-weight bag in one of your garages and whale. You'll surprise yourself, and it'll be good for Willliam. Dude, you're at work all day, and if I were a betting man, I'd lay odds Lissa was impatient with the kids, maybe not all of them, but her first one. Her parents probably made her do the mail-order bride thing because they couldn't afford her, and there wasn't a good prospect for marriage in her area. I speculate she's from a small town or village in Viet Nam. Lots of poverty there."

Trinity suffered through Lissa's conceit and condescending attitude, but being the baby of seven, she could throw it right back. The beautiful Creole girl was not one to trifle with; she more than knew how to take up for herself. The way the woman spoke about Mays pissed her off beyond words, and she'd just about had her fill when the two men walked in the door.

"We had a good hike, saw a doe and her fawns, then followed with a good jog. Mays held stride with me the whole time. It felt good to be with someone that understood me. Can we get some water?" Sweat poured off both men; Mays threw him a handtowel, wiping his face with another.

Lissa's eyes shot daggers, "Are those from the powder room? Do you know how much they cost?" Mays cast a glance at Babe, then back at Lissa.

"I don't care, I bought the motherfuckers and you can buy more." Trinity almost fell out of the chair. Babe's face was priceless. In one morning's walk, his straight-laced brother had crossed to the motherfucking world of his brother. She held back a laugh. Miss Prime and Proper bitch with a haughty attitude wasn't quite sure what to make of it. "We're going in the steam and sauna. Why don't you join us? I'm pretty sure one of your swimsuits will work for Trinity." The woman was still speechless after Mays' comment. The influences of her man ran through her head.

"Mays, you mind if I use your washer? According to Trinity, my shirt would be funk-nasty." They chuckled, and Lissa offered to take it for him. "No, ma'am, you don't need to wait on me, but you can lead the way." Both men took off their shirts. With his lily-white jelly stomach, Mays starkly contrasted Babe's olive skin color and shredded muscles. His older brother was curious about the tats. Babe was more than happy to explain the significance of each. Like most people, Mays wanted to hear combat stories. Surprisingly, Babe started to tell him one she'd heard as they walked into the steam room.

Lissa turned the corner and had three bathing suits that Trinity could try on. "This will be fine. Thank you." She braided her hair to the side, hoping it wouldn't become unmanageable. "I'll wait for you," she told her sister-in-law. "I know Mays doesn't talk like that, but Babe has an influence on other people's language, trust me. You oughta hear when he talks to his Marine buddies, but it's part of him and certainly not meant to cause waves. Not saying I'm a saint by a long shot, but some of the things that come out his mouth are jaw-dropping."

When the women entered the steam room, the brothers were in an intense conversation about Babe's life as a Marine. Trinity feared it would awaken nightmares and was leery he'd have a spell. Trinity's mind flashed; if Lissa had been shocked by the language, invisible people and non-existent combats would likely push her over the edge.

They sat quietly and listened to the guys talk. Mays was in awe of what Babe had done and the idea of threats of life or death matters. "Lis? Babe and Trinity are going to Norway in a month or so, and they asked if we wanted to go."

"Sure, but what about the kids?'

Mays was quick to answer, "They can stay with my parents. I'm sure they would love it." He glanced toward Babe. "Hey, would you like to meet my mom and dad? I also have two sisters, both adopted but not from the same situation, thank God. They were babies. One is seven years younger, and the other eight years younger, which puts them closer to your age. I'm ten years older than you, right? I'm forty-eight, shit, almost to the half-century mark."

They decided to meet Mays' mom and dad the following day. The outburst from Mays seemed to knock the bitch out of Lissa, making her far more pleasant. While the day had been action-packed and created much conversation, they burned for some alone time.

Even though the day had started rough overhearing Lissa's temper tantrum or abusive behavior, it all settled down, especially after Mays' uncharacteristic blurt. Trinity wasn't necessarily fond of her new sister-in-law but figured there must've been a story behind Lissa's unusual snobbery. Mays was anything but snobbish.

They Ubered back to the hotel, and despite Mays' offered ride, they needed time together. "Babe, don't get me wrong, and I hope this doesn't piss you off, but it's almost like being back at Louie's, ya know, no time alone. I get the significance of this visit, but I want one day or even half a day to just lay in bed with you, order room service, and not have to put a speck of clothing on our bodies. I want to touch you, climb in your lap, and kiss you whenever without feeling like there is an audience." She could see the wheels turning in his head. He gazed into her eyes, cradled the back of her neck, and brought her in for a heat-filled kiss.

"How about we have breakfast in bed and meet Mays and company around three? That gives us time with him and their kids and then meeting his parents. Do you know how often I asked myself why they didn't put me up for adoption, but my relationship with my grandfather was second to none? I resented having the parents I had but not the grands. The whole thing is fucked, and it's all because of Gino, not my mother. Old, decrepit, whatever he might be, he is going to pay for Mays' hearing impairment, and I know just how I'm gonna do it." He had an evil, almost demonic deviance in his eyes. Trinity found his obvious thrill of planning a fantasy murder most disturbing. She couldn't blame him for being angry, but actually planning on killing someone was a different kind of scary crazy.

She held his hand as they got out of the Uber. Even though the driver had put in ear pods after the kiss, she felt he probably could hear some of Babe's commentary. The big guy appeared unbothered by any of his thoughts. She stayed quiet. They stopped at the restaurant and looked the menu over. "That crab salad looks good." She tapped on the glass protecting the menu.

"My girl, I'd advise you to avoid any seafood or descriptions that say New Orleans style anything. You'll be sorely disappointed. Now lobster is different; I suppose it's good at any top-rated restaurant if you want surf and turf."

"Oh, what about the sausage?" She pointed to a description of an andouille dish despite Babe's warning.

Babe tickled her ribs, laughing. "I was hoping you might go for that," he said with a smile.

Her eyes widened, and her cheeks took on a blush. "Babe Vicarelli, I can't believe you said that out loud." She slapped his arm. "I saw what I want, and you?"

"Oh, yeah, I see what I want." He pushed his finger into her armpit, soliciting a squeal. Like two kids, they made a fast pace to the bank of elevators. "For being a honeymoon of sorts, we've had way too many deep conversations. All play tonight. No serious talk. Deal?" He asked with a double lift of his brows.

"Yes, sir!" She saluted him. When they got off the elevator and to the room, he backed her toward the bed.

As planned, they lazed in each other's arms for most of the morning, having breakfast in bed. Even though it was chilly by New Orleans standards, they had the air conditioner blowing cold, playing like kids underneath the covers. She teased him about how he'd gone from a silent mystery to open and accessible. Trinity was honest about how casually, almost euphorically, he referenced offing Gino.

"You can't say things like that; I mean, if I said 'I'm gonna kill Bob Smith,' you'd know it was an expression. It's not like I'd really do it, but you sounded sincere about Gino, and it wigged me a little or maybe a lot." He grabbed her waist and rolled her on top of him, nuzzling his face between her breasts, muffling the words, 'Nothing serious.'

Babe and Trinity's phones dinged at the same time.

> Mays: What time are you coming here?
> Babe: 3
> Mays: Work out? I've been waiting
> Babe: Sure. 2 work better?
> Mays: Whatever works for you and Trinity
> Babe: See u at 2

Trinity cocked her head as he put the phone down. "So y'all gonna go on a long-ass walk again?" She unconsciously stuck her bottom lip out in a full-blown pout.

Babe scooped her up, laying her on the bed. He flipped the television to a paid movie channel. The new Top Gun was the feature film, but he waited for her approval before he selected play. Leaning back against the headboard, which was tufted leather affixed to the wall, she crawled into the crook of his arm. She kissed the scar made by being shot in combat. He focused down at her, saying it was a minor inconvenience. She slid the covers down, examining the more recent scar, which still had not healed fully. She kissed it, laughing, saying all his boo-boos had been kissed better. As she kissed his hip, his mind flipped back to Carmen and his disappointment with himself. *To tell or not? Not, at least, not now.*

Both became engrossed in the movie, and it was one-thirty by the time it ended—no time for a quick shower. Babe threw on workout clothes; she slipped into jeans and a loose-fitting cotton sweater. She grabbed his jeans and long-sleeve Henley, stuffed them in her shoulder bag, and bolted for the elevator. Catching a cab, they headed for Mays. He texted that they were on the way.

When they arrived at the house, Mays greeted them at the door, dressed in newly purchased wicking workout attire and bright white running shoes. He bounced from side to side like a child needing the potty, not quite a boxer in the ring. Lissa was nowhere in sight; he commented she was taking a nap, but for Trinity to make herself at home. *Odd.*

Babe kissed her sweetly, saying they wouldn't be that long. Trinity plopped on the sofa and started scrolling through her phone. She'd missed a call from Bethany, so she promptly returned the call.

"You rang?"

"Sorry, I know it's your honeymoon, but I needed to talk. Look, I'm not telling you to come home by any means, but I knew you'd be upset if I—"

"What's wrong?" She felt her heart race in fear. "Mama, Daddy?"

"No, it's Chance. He got mugged, and they beat him pretty bad and stole his watch and diamond ring." Trinity gasped and could feel her bottom lip begin to quiver. *Hold it together.* "Daddy has Big Paul looking for the guys. There were three of them against poor Chance. The court recently released them from O.P.P. for the same thing. Daddy's mad as a hornet; you wouldn't believe how angry he is. It's like when you—" Bethany's voice cracked. "I didn't mean to say that; I'm sorry."

"First flight home tomorrow. I can't believe it. Where was he? Oh, never mind. I'll see you as soon as possible. Don't tell Mama, then she'll be worried about us. Thanks for calling me, and yes, I woulda been totally pissed. Love you."

"Love you, Trinity." They hung up.

She swallowed hard as bile pushed up her throat, knowing if Big Paul didn't find them, Babe would when they got home. The thought crossed her mind that her dad might even involve her man. *God, I hope not.* Trinity decided to make herself at home since the hostess was napping. *Bizarre.* She grabbed a Diet Coke out of the fridge.

Lissa stumbled into the kitchen, past sloppy drunk. Trinity couldn't help but think, *Wow, Houston, we have a problem.* With slurred words, she advised Trinity not to go to Mays' parents' house, mumbling something to the effect that they were racist and would probably have a problem with her skin color. Then she whispered since she was African American.

"I'm French Haitian." She corrected. Lissa said it didn't matter; all they cared about was that she wasn't white. Her mind was on Chance and how Babe would react to that news, and Lord help them if Mays' parents showed any disrespect. Thoughts pinged through her head; maybe they didn't like Lissa since she was abusive to their son, or an alcoholic, or probably hoity-toity to them. None of those options would be surprising. Yes, there was a story there, but the ending thus far had been ugly.

Trinity heard the front door open and watched Lissa sneak into the hallway and probably back to bed.

"Ready to hit some weights or the heavy bag?" Mays had changed in one encounter with Babe. *Oh, my.* His face was bright pink and sweaty. "I kept up with your hubby," he proudly announced to Trinity. Babe's eyes jetted toward hers.

"What's wrong, ma girl?" His brows furrowed with a deep frown.

Tears began to fill her eyes, "Chance was mugged and beaten pretty bad. Three thugs the courts had released from O.P.P. Can you believe it?" He held her. "I'm sorry, but I have to leave tomorrow. You can stay—"

"No fuckin' way. I've seen the punks. If it's who I think it is, it was the night Clive came to Louie's." He looked apologetically at Mays, "Sorry, my brotha, we gotta get back to the city. Think about Norway. We will keep in touch, but we gotta blow right now." They hugged. "Keep up the working out. Next time I see you, I expect to see a difference. Remember, we have the same blood. Hanging out has been unbelievable, thank you. Apologize to your mom and dad. We will be in touch; you have my word."

APPOINTED TIME

*A*ntoine paced behind his desk, picked up his water bottle, and threw it across the room. "Rose Marie," he pressed the speaker to her phone. "Call Big Paul and call my sons to the office." He mumbled under his breath. For a man of complete composure, he had abandoned all sense of control. He barked orders. His secretary of many years had never seen him so rattled. The police department and judicial system had let him down. For years, he and his family before him remembered them handsomely at all fundraisers and holidays, taking care of their families in times of need.

They let him down, and now his youngest son was fighting for his life. A cracked skull created intracranial swelling, and he lay motionless like the dead. There were more wires and tubes attached to his son, and the doctor's prognosis wasn't comforting; if anything, it was discouraging. There was barely any brain activity. The only diminutive comment seemed to reflect his being young and healthy. If praying the Rosary or hailing prayers to God and Mother Mary was the answer, Antoinette had that more than covered. Antoine didn't function well in limbo, where his snap of the fingers didn't produce results.

His phone buzzed, it was Big Paul. "Sir, we are scouring every inch of the city. I have men everywhere. No word yet. Who's responsible for the release of the three? Maybe a conversation with them might be in order. The situation is an abomination, and somebody will pay, Antoine. Have no fear."

Trinity's panic regarding her brother left no room for flight worries. With legs crossed, her foot-shaking was enough to ignite sparks. "Woman, settle down. We will get this sorted out."

Ignorant of the severity of Chance's injuries, Trinity imagined a black eye, maybe a few scrapes, a broken nose or jaw. Had she any idea of the tightrope he was tiptoeing between life and death, there would be no consolation. The siblings were all close, but Trinity had a special bond with Chance, maybe because they were closer in age and both had broken many of the rules. The first five were rule followers, straight-A students, polite, and stayed far from the misfits or fray of humanity, whereas she and Chance broke the rules and, like insects to light, they were magnets drawn to the wild, live on the edge, perhaps even black sheep of society. They thrived in controversy and dramatics, but for all their monkey business, they were the two most outgoing and flamboyant in personality. Neither had ever met a stranger and were deemed the life of the party.

Closing her eyes, she could visualize when the two of them went on a rolling spree. They thought they'd gotten away with it and quietly returned to the house, whispering as they made it to the stairs, the living room table lamp illuminated. Dressed in her house coat and silk head scarf, Mama Noelle cleared her throat, "Trinity Marie, Chance Nathaniel, come here this minute! Not only will you apologize to our neighbors, but you will clean all the paper up and work until you can pay for all the rolls of toilet tissue you wasted. Get to bed, and don't wake anyone in the process." The memory must have washed a smile on her face because Babe commented.

"Chance and I used to cut up something fierce. Our parents, mostly Mama, had a time with us. We could always make her laugh, but she didn't hesitate to punish us or threaten the belt. I think she may have used a hairbrush once, but never the belt, but boy, she threatened it. The other kids were never, ever in trouble." She became silent and thoughtful for a second, "God, I hope his face didn't get scarred. He's so pretty, and I know I shouldn't call him pretty, but he is."

The flight home seemed far shorter to her than going there, and it wasn't nearly as scary. It was amazing to see the power of an occupied mind. It had only been a few days, and yet it seemed like Babe and Mays had known each other much longer, like growing up together closeness. At first, he was skeptical, but Mays' warm and welcoming personality broke down any barriers Babe had built. It was because he desperately wanted a family. Yes, he was a loner and, from all appearances, functioned well. The heart from his childhood had cocooned itself because there was no other way to survive. Babe wasn't one to attach to people, yet the man who was his brother grabbed his heart and knocked down the walls of vulnerability. Trinity had encouraged him to stay in Atlanta, and she'd go home by herself, but she knew he'd never go for it, and he didn't.

Once they landed, got their bags, and were headed for Hotel Noelle, Babe called Antoine. "Sir, we have landed in New Orleans and are on our way to you. I heard about Chance's misfortune. I'm fairly certain I know the trio if it's who I think it is. One white and two Latinos? I can't believe they released them. I've gotten them once, but there were bystanders. Next time will be the last."

Trinity was texting fast and furiously and began to sob. She called Bethany, asking what she meant by it was terrible. Hand supporting her head, she listened intently. It was incomprehensible to think Chance may not make it. All she wanted at that moment was to see her brother. He called Antoine back to let him know Trinity wanted to see Chance, but he'd join in the effort to locate the bastards and bring them to justice.

Their desks butted up to each other. Trey was busy with his clickety-click pen reading over statements while Max reran video footage from Louie's. "What a piece of shit, the loudmouth from Louie's? The asshole who punched you. I'm watching him muscle through the crowd and harass patrons to get to the bar, elbowing his way through. Here it is: Finn brings him a drink while Trinity mean mugs the dude. Oh fuck. The Hulk walks behind him, says something to Trinity, then turns and walks away. Nothing is happening. People shove him from both sides. What a piece of work. Wait, this must be when it happens. A guy says something pushes him into a woman who starts going bazonkers. Sometime during the push and shove, the guy gets shivved."

Trey looked him in the face with a pan expression and commented about Babe's presence and how it always appeared to be a coincidence. Trey moved around the desk, telling Max to rerun it but to slow the speed. Both watched intently; they saw the big guy's jaw movement, confirming he was saying something to Trinity, who turned her head in his direction. Then he leaves. The shoving continues for five minutes. Then, after a final rough shoulder slam, the man falls into a woman who starts screaming. "You're right, Max, The Hulk is long gone. My bet would be on the last guy or someone in the crowd. It's pretty tight. I don't get what his deal is or was with Trinity. She's friendly, makes great drinks, and is fast as lightning. We can pass by this evening before calling it a day. See if she remembers anything, but the big guy wasn't involved."

The drive to Touro seemed to take forever; all she could do was think about was how to react when she arrived. Even though her heart was broken, being in control was more critical. It wasn't about her. Traffic moved at a snail's pace, aggravating her more and more. "What the fuck is wrong with these people," she yelled. "C'mon people, drive your fucking car. Babe, is it me, or is every Scooby on the road today?"

Not gonna answer that one. "Traffic is moving slower than usual." *Bullshit. Yes, Trinity, it is you.* "Want me to drop you at the door and then park?" She shook her head no.

He wasted not a moment parking the car and getting to the ICU. Bethany and Louis were in the waiting area. Bethany raced to her side; both sisters clung to each other. Louis shook Babe's hand. He mentioned they were taking turns at the hospital, but their mother had never left. They wanted to make sure someone was there when he woke up. The missing *if* was deafening. Bethany held Trinity's hand and, with a somber tone, went through the list of injuries he had sustained, then concluded the doctors said the odds were not in his favor to regain consciousness. Trinity's breath stifled; the pains in her chest started just like when everyone thought Babe was dead. She let her mother's words roll through her head. *"You're not having a heart attack; more like a panic attack. What were you thinking about?"* She let out one held-back sob. She'd never had anyone close to her die. She hadn't been close to Mere; she was too young to remember much. Papere had died before she was born. Being the youngest child in the family, she'd missed out on the grandparent bond. She brushed those thoughts aside; they were nothing to dwell on. Chance was going to get better. Trinity reached into her purse and folded her hands in prayer, holding each bead of her Rosary. She sat silently with closed eyes.

Before long, Antoinette stepped into the waiting room. Seeing her baby girl, she held out her arms and hugged her tightly, whispering she needed to see Chance. Trinity must have asked if Babe could go with her, but her mother shook her head, raising a finger to say one at a time.

Someone from the ICU walked her back to Chance's room. A symphony of beeps, muffled air movement, and whirring monitors filled the air. It was almost serene—a stillness she had never known. The medical team had shaved a large section of his hair, and there were staples along two incisions in his head. His face was bruised and cut. An intubation device protruded from his mouth and was connected to a machine that breathed for him. The man in the bed resembled her brother, but it didn't seem like him. She touched his hand. A few tears trickled down her face. She whispered, "Chance, I want you to get better. You have to, but I'll be okay if God has other ideas. Don't you worry none; Babe is gonna take care of these people that done you this. I don't want you to suffer. You'll always be my brother." Was she the only one in the family that knew he was dying? He wasn't going to get better. It would take a Jesus Lazarus moment for him to get better. If they hadn't already, her family needed to let him know it was okay for him to go. She kissed the top of his hand and told him she loved him. She walked back to the waiting room. It was then that she saw everyone knew, as well. They had waited for her to get home and held quiet about the situation until there was understanding in her heart.

Within the next half hour, all family members filled the waiting room. Her heart tore when her father walked in. Jaws clenched, eyes misty with unfallen tears, Antoine was composed. Trinity could no longer hold back when he held her mother, and tears fell, accompanied by shudders of silent sobs. Her mother and father together created a force of strength encompassing the room. They had already had moments of tears and stoically braved the inevitable together. One by one, each family member bid farewell, with her parents being the last as they left the room. Chance had been brain-dead. The surgeons tried every approach but to no avail. All that was left was to wait for Trinity, and now that she was home, they could let him go in peace. They headed straight to St. Dominic's, where Father O'Shea met them.

The good Father had words of kindness and compassion. Babe and Antoine exchanged several glances. Each time, the big guy respectfully nodded with an almost undetectable tip of his head—no utterances needed. Antoine had given him a mission, one he would complete. Big Paul had been searching for the trio of thugs, but Babe knew what they looked like and would carry out justice. He didn't need help.

There wasn't much to talk about, and all the wonderful things happening in their life suddenly paled and seemed inconsequential. A few blocks from St. Dominic, The Steak Knife had been one of their family's favorite places to dine. The families had known each other for decades. Since it was late, Antoine called ahead, and the family graciously opened their arms and said they'd stay as long as he needed. Father O'Shea joined them. Trinity didn't think she'd ever be happy again. Her heart ached, and it seemed like a bad dream, but it wasn't. Now she understood why Babe questioned a loving God. Right then, she doubted God.

"Babe, I get your questions about God. Right now, I can't believe He would take my brother. My chest is tight, and my heart feels crushed; I can hardly breathe. I wish they would've told me. We could have come back earlier. Oh my God, thank Heavens, you refused to stay. Did you know?" She turned in the seat, looking at him, "Did you?" Suddenly, she was furious and conjured ideas that had no substance. She imagined a family member called him and told him Chance was dying, but to keep it from her. Or maybe Babe knew, and that's why he didn't stay in Atlanta. She turned away from him, refusing to speak. "Babe, let me out of the truck; I'll walk to the restaurant."

He pulled over and locked the doors and windows. "You are not getting out, and of course, I didn't know, how could I? Trinity, if your dad or anyone had called me, I would have passed the phone to you. I would never keep anything from you. I am telling you this, I'm gonna kill the motherfuckers, and you can take that to the bank. I wanna find out what judge cut them loose. Believe me; heads are going to roll on this." He pulled her to him, lifting her over the console. She sat in his lap like a child. She repeated over and over how she wanted to hurt someone. "I get it, my girl. Don't abandon your faith right now. You're angry, and it's all a part of the grief process. Your whole family has to go through it."

She leaned against him and mumbled, "If it's a boy, I want to name him Chance. Is that okay?"

"Of course. Anything but Babe. Let's walk from here."

For days, Trinity walked around like she was dead. There was no dancing at Louie's; all she wanted to do was stay in bed. Babe gave her some leeway and told Ruthie to do the same. The boys walked on eggshells around her.

The funeral felt more like a celebration of life, even though his life was snatched way too soon. It was well-attended; shocked seemed to be the descriptive term of the day, and rightfully so. No one expressed it aloud, but the underlying current was, who would be so stupid to kill Antoine Noelle's son? They had to be from out of town or didn't realize who they had beaten to death. Everyone knew the killer would discover the gross mistake the hard way. Like any Noelle affair, the drinks flowed freely, and the food was endless.

Trey approached Babe and said, "What a sorry state of affairs. You know who did it?" He raised one eyebrow. "It's fucked up. We do our job, and then the judicial system lets them loose to do it again. Mind you, Marine, we'll get them. There's been an APB since it happened. Lowlifes like that eventually show their face. They get too cocky and bold. When they do, we'll be waiting for them." Babe listened and shook his head, but inside, he knew the police wouldn't get a chance. It was going to be a killing spree—the three degenerates and the most despicable piece of shit to walk the earth, motherfucking Gino Vicarelli. He knew exactly how he was going to kill him.

Max tapped Babe on the shoulder. "You and Trinity got married, and we didn't get an invite? If it weren't for us, you would've never gotten the nerve to talk to your Creole Blossom." He sipped from a water bottle.

"What, no Diet Coke? You're right; I should have invited y'all, then I would've had two more people on my side of the aisle." He threw a half smile.

Max jingled the change or keys in one of his pockets. He wasn't comfortable and knew the system had let the Noelles down. "How's your girl?" Babe shook his head and bit his lower lip, closing his eyes. "Nuff said. Hey, can I ask you something? Don't think I'm being insulting, no. Is she—" Max stepped back to avoid a chuck on the arm if he was wrong.

"Pregnant? Yes. In a couple of weeks, we will find out what model we get, one with or without. Trey's wife has to have had the baby by now. Everything okay?"

Trey moved in quickly, flashed his phone, and swiped through a ton of pictures. "It looks like she's gonna be a blonde like her mom. Presley Jane is a week and a half old and has a set of lungs. She has her days and nights mixed up. I have to tip-toe around the house. Lord help me if I wake her up."

Trinity walked up and said hello to Trey and Max. They offered condolences; she politely thanked them, pulling Babe by the arm. They excused themselves. She needed to be held. He engulfed her, pulling her close and kissing the top of her head. It wasn't that she wanted to talk; she just wanted to be left alone, and for the most part, very few people approached Babe.

Over the next week, Babe kept his attention on the news for robberies. Maybe the assholes wouldn't hit the Quarter right away, but they might start a spree in other areas, like college town. For the most part, students at Loyola and Tulane drove nice rides and came from money. Easy targets, for sure. Another option was Magazine Street with all the shops but more than likely someone with an armful of groceries or kids—easy pickings for assholes like that.

It wasn't long before he heard of a few robberies around college town. Since Trinity was staying home and away from Louie's, he could do his running in the evening before dinner or late at night after everyone was asleep.

The mood was solemn on the construction site. The workers mroved at a slower pace. *This needs rectifying.* Even though most of the crew had no clue who Chance was, they knew the owner's horrible story. Glenn paced the trailer as Gunn and Babe entered. He nodded at the big man and sat for some Gunner attention. The scene was worthy of a professional photo. Glenn had his forehead against the dog, both looking eye to eye. A single tear rolled down Glenn's cheek. He sat up, stroking the fur along his four-legged friend's head down his back.

"Vic, you doing okay? How's Trinity?" He looked away. "Bethany is a mess, hell, so am I. Antoine is the strongest man I know. I can't fathom the enormity of sadness they must be feeling." He pulled out a wrinkled handkerchief, wiped his eyes, and blew his nose.

Babe put on his hard hat and spoke a single word. "Time." He left the trailer, walking to the action point of the site. Imparting instruction, he reviewed a list of things that needed attention. "Any questions?" He waited a few seconds, surmising, "Didn't think so."

As he worked, thoughts of Gino battered around, posing questions. Did he still live in Mid-City? Was he still a regular at the neighborhood bar, if it was even there anymore? There was no doubt how he'd make him pay for Mays' hearing loss. The fantasy started building a throbbing heat below the belt. Why did the rush of taking a life cause the same reaction as bringing ultimate pleasure? He'd have to look up interviews with serial killers; maybe it was a common thread. Javier had been right. It was the best description of his need. He needed to pay retribution for their actions. Would offing the mugger, killer trio, and Gino's execution be righteous kills? There had to be such a thing, right? There was so much he needed to ponder. He knew one hundred percent it was breaking one of the Top Ten in God's rule book. Maybe once the baby was born, he'd hang up his mission. The job then would be to raise a caring, loving, responsible human, not pass on the monster of darkness.

Gunner bounded up to him. "What's up?" The dog looked back at the office trailer and then back at Babe. He repeated it with a bark in between. "Okay, okay, let's go see." When they entered the trailer, Glenn was sitting on the floor, a bottle of whiskey by his side. His face was red, and patterns of dried tears streaked his face. "Glenn, you okay?"

"No. Vic, can I tell you something just between us?" Babe pulled up a chair, grabbed Glenn's arm, and moved him into the other seat. "I saw the guys a few times passing by the site. They were across the street, not like casing our work or anything. They passed, minding their business. I remember you telling me to be on the lookout. I should have called the police. That's one thing, and I was supposed to meet Chance at a club on Bourbon. I don't know if he was cutting through an alley or on a dark side street; I didn't have the balls to ask where they found his body. The point is, he was coming to meet me. It's my fault." He started sobbing. "I can't tell Bethany or any of the Noelles."

Babe leaned forward, resting his arms on his knees. "No, you can't. Take this for what it's worth; it resonated with me, and since then, I've accepted death, period. You might be sad because you miss the person, but here's the thing. In training, going for my first jump, the instructor said, 'No need to fear death; everyone will one day meet it, so why worry.' My point to you is it was Chance's time. He could have canceled with you, gone a different route, or gotten waylaid at work. No, it was his appointed time. I wouldn't say that to Bethany or anyone else, but I'm sharing it with you. No matter what, it would have happened one way or another." Glenn's jaw had dropped, and he looked in wonder at Babe.

"That's why you're never afraid of anything?"

The big guy replied he couldn't claim that as fact. Anything to do with Trinity was a different kettle of fish, but he knew even that thought was irrational. He reiterated everyone had their personal appointed time.

After the counseling session with Glenn, the day moved forward; before long, it was quitting time.

PAYBACK IS A

Rather than going home from work, Babe drove down Canal Street toward Mid-City. He turned on Carrollton Avenue. Navigating the narrow side streets, he hung a right, passing by his old house on Bienville. It just so happened Gino was out front, spiffed as much as possible for his decrepit self and heading to his favorite watering hole, Liuzza's. Parked at the house was an old blue Buick with a broken taillight; it looked like something the piece of shit would drive. The conquest of Gino was going to be a piece of cake. No rush there. Babe remembered which window to enter through, and he'd lay in wait. He'd have to wear his work gloves or find some Latex that was big enough. No prints, period.

First on his agenda of righting wrongs was the trio of thugs. He made the block and meandered toward Carrollton toward Walmsley, winding around and ultimately landing on Broadway. A late-night run in college town would suit his needs. He'd start on Freret Street, hitting several blocks, half on the streets behind the frat houses and the rest on the other side of Broadway, past the ritzy streets near the library. He'd find the motherfuckers and have no mercy. He had a nine-inch billy club, but something more substantial might be in order, like his baton. While he preferred hands-on and a cervical splintering torque, his M.O. had become a topic of curiosity—not an option. Running into them would be a miracle, and he didn't think it would be appropriate to ask God.

After circling the blocks, getting a clearer lay of the land, shadowy spots, and areas of concealment, everything would have to be quick.

Silencing them was of utmost importance. In the case of a passerby, he had to cover any distinguishing marks, like the ink on his body. Ticking over in his mind was what he'd wear—Black Henley from Javier, the one with the bullet hole, his black joggers, and his favorite sleeveless hoodie. Since he ran every day, it wouldn't be alarming to Ruthie, Trinity, or the boys. It would take patience and diligence on his part.

He pulled into the driveway; Ruthie was sitting on the porch waiting for him. *What have they done now?* It was all he could think. They made eye contact. Her posture didn't indicate anything awry, but the old gal was a tough bird. "You running late today. Everything okay?"

"I was about to ask you the same thing. Just enjoying the breeze, or have the boys been acting up? Talking back? Fighting?" He sat next to her on a wicker bench. The creaks and give in the weave gave a feeling like he was about to fall through. "Maybe we better sit on something more solid." He stood and leaned against the wall. Narrowing his eyes about to speak, she spoke first.

"We had a strange occurrence. Someone came by the house today; I answered it, but the person said they had the wrong house and walked away. You think someone's looking to break in? Ya know, Mister Rune has a security system, but he never used it. I'm thinking maybe we should start. Your girl, I mean, wife, and I are both here all day except I run a few errands now and then; she's still lying in bed." She folded her hands in her lap. "Not trying to tell you your business, but that's not good for her or your baby." She pulled a Kleenex from up her sleeve and wiped her nose. "Darn allergies, something must be a-blooming. Dinner has another half-hour in the oven; it'll give you time to shower." *Not that you want to tell me my business,* he laughed inside. "Sorry to bother you when ya just getting home, but I thought it was important for you to know." He nodded, held the door open for her, and followed inside. The boys were dutifully doing homework. She had them well-trained.

Jacob handed him a paper. The gloat on his face was unmistakable. "A+, big guy." *Big guy?* "How you like dem apples?"

With a slight tick upward of his smile, he answered, "Dem apples? Boy, where you hear that shit? A+, I'd say, excellent. Now that I know you can do it, I expect to see more of those." He handed the paper back.

Jacob groaned, "Gimme a f—" Babe cocked his head. "Freakin' break. School's hard, and I feel lucky to get an A." The boy cocked up one side of his lip, disgusted. "Ask Reg how he did on the science test." He snickered, held up one hand as a barrier, and flicked him off with the other.

Reg rolled his eyes, cocked his head at Jacob. His expression was equivalent to, 'That's your ass.' He dug papers from the bookbag and handed them to Babe.

"Well done, Reg. Not too shabby, you studied hard for this test. Keep up the good work."

Jacob threw both his hands up. "What the fuck? He got a fuckin B. I got an A+." Ruthie's grumble was loud enough to hear from the kitchen. Jacob popped up and stuck his head in the kitchen, "Sorry, Miss Ruthie. Do I have to go to my room?"

She turned slightly with her hand on her hip, "No, just put fifty cents in the jar."

"Yes, ma'am," he said sadly under his breath and dropped two quarters in the four-letter word jar. Usually, the f-bomb required room time, and the lesser evils called for fifty cents, sometimes a quarter or a dollar. It was all in the circumstances.

Babe leaned on the table after Jacob returned and whispered, "Listen, you little motherfuckers, watch your mouth around Ruthie. I'll be down for dinner. Go play hoops or something for the next half hour if schoolwork is complete." They scrambled to pack up their bookbags and scatter into the yard. Babe walked through the kitchen, deposited a five in the jar, and continued to Trinity.

She sat cross-legged on the bed in her Saints shorts and tank with a large picture book on the bed. He sat and kissed her. Glancing at the photo album, he saw scads of pictures of Trinity with her siblings growing up. She'd removed a stack. He flipped through them. They were all of her and Chance. They looked similar, both having finer, more European features. All of the Noelle offspring were beautiful people.

"How's my girl today? What you been up to?" He hugged her close, drawing in an elongated breath as he inhaled the scent of her hair. "Patchouli? So, I know you showered today and reminisced down memory lane with the photos. What else?"

"Slept, read, why, was I supposed to be doing something?" She sounded off-put, borderline rude.

"Nope. I'm getting in the shower; dinner will be ready in about fifteen." He knew she was hurting, but he didn't need to feel the brunt of her anger. He understood. An idea switched on like a light; he took her hand and pulled her out of the bed. "Come with me." She was resistant but complied. He walked her downstairs, into the garage, and handed her Jacob's punching gloves. He took her hands and fastened them on her. "Whale away," he said, pointing to the heavyweight bag. She pushed it with a light bump of her fist—zero energy. "Again," he ordered.

Trinity rolled her eyes, "This is stupid," and rocked the bag again.

"Are you mad? Is there someone you'd like to hurt? Or is everything sunshine and roses?" He taunted.

"Fuck you, Vic," she glared at him.

"Well?" That was all the encouragement she needed, inspiring her to let loose. Like a wild woman, she threw hard punches and kicks, yelling as she sobbed. She worked the bag. After ten minutes, she threw her arms around him and cried. "Feel any relief? It's only temporary, but the bag is here twenty-four-seven and at your disposal. If the boys are on it, move them off. You have dibs."

When they returned inside, everyone was sitting with their plates in front of them, obviously waiting on Babe and Trinity. Dinner consisted of lasagna and salad. The boys looked at the big square of the Italian delight. They looked at anything to avoid eye contact with Trinity. Ruthie broke the silence. "Chris, it's your turn to say grace." He complied.

The silence at the table returned, creating an uncomfortable icyness. The boys didn't know what to say, so they stayed quiet. Trinity commented on the lasagna, and everyone else jumped in to agree it was delicious. The conversation was forced and awkward.

"Boys," Babe said, "Trinity knows y'all are sorry that her brother died. You don't need to watch your words or treat her any differently. It's okay for y'all to talk, laugh, and be your obnoxious selves. Jacob's paper earned him an A+, and Reg received a B on his science test to keep you up to speed," he informed Trinity. She smiled. "Chris, any grades we need to hear about? It's most important to keep your marks high for college, being a senior now. How's it looking?"

Chris said he had a three-point four average, and his last ACT was a twenty-five, but he would retake it. He understood he'd need to keep it up if he expected to get into LSU. College conversation continued for the next half hour and appeared to help bring life back into Trinity's demeanor. She wanted to know what made him want to go to Baton Rouge. The other two laughed, exclaiming Brooke. "Don't choose a college for a girl, just my advice. Girls will come and go, and you'll be at a university you don't want to be at. You have any other friends going?" Trinity asked.

He looked at her as though it was an insane question to ask. "Most of my class is going to LSU. I'll know a lot of people there. I haven't decided if I want to rush. You, know, fraternity stuff?" His tone was condescending.

Babe fired back, not wanting to take the wind out of the boy's sail but perhaps take him down a peg or two. He started to sound as snotty as Brooke, who was from money. Maybe Babe's bank account and investments amounted to a sizeable sum; he still considered himself a devil dog and didn't need all the fineries he could afford. "Chris, do you have reference letters for any fraternities? Rushing requires recommendations. Also, does Brooke know you plan on going to LSU to be with her? Just cause you're shtucking the girl doesn't mean she wants you at college with her. High school is a different thing." Chris looked confused. "We'll talk after dinner." He could see Ruthie did not think it was table talk. Trinity tried to hold back her laughter, which sounded like the garbage disposal, giving everyone at the table a chuckle, even Ruthie.

A few hours after they finished dinner with all down for the night, Babe kissed Trinity and said he was off for a run. "You need to put something on with reflectors, or no one will see you." He kissed her again, saying he'd be fine.

Once outside, he reached into the truck and grabbed his baton. At sixteen inches, he stuck part in his pants and hid it inside his hoodie. After ten minutes of stretching, he was off down Chestnut to Calhoun, taking a right and going several blocks to St. Charles Avenue. There was barely any traffic, but he knew the closer he got to the campuses, the more activity would be stirring. Eyes alert, he continued on Calhoun to Freret and turned left. There was a group of three people headed his way. He stopped pretending to tie his shoe. It was three drunk college kids, not his mark. Continuing to Broadway, he jogged in place, waiting for a few cars to pass before crossing. The run took him down to Pine. Question: Go right toward Willow or left? Either way, the street was dark, so he opted to go right to Willow, then down to Calhoun, retracing his steps until he was home. *Maybe tomorrow night.*

Trinity was sound asleep. He showered and climbed into bed. Instinctively, she cuddled next to him. Her belly was definitely growing. The baby bump had become pronounced. Her purring breaths sent him straight to sleep.

Five o'clock rolled around; he got in a workout and shower. The steam clouded the glass doors. Rolling his head in circles under the shower, he heard Taps playing. He thought the illusory shit had ended, but no, trickles of heartbreaking voices filled with hate and disdain enveloped him.

Incoming. Incoming. High-pitched shrills echoed through the sky. The sickening smell of charred flesh filled his nostrils. The chaos of people running amidst bellows of commands, blood-curdling screams of pain, and sorrowful pleas for help penetrated his ears. His brain likened the feeling to screwdrivers puncturing his eardrums. What? It hadn't happened yet. The ghosts were merging into his plans. *Blood started flushing under the glass shower door. 'Cap, help,' he heard the pitiful cry. It felt like someone was trying to shove their way into his space. He leaned back, holding it in steady. Swirl patterns in the marble shower wall randomly moved like a psychedelic trip. Reality faded, and he was immersed in Taliban territory. Brewster's arm, torn from his elbow, left a stump pulsing blood. The rhythmic thuds of copter blades pierced through the agony surrounding him with a hand reaching out to grab his. 'C'mon Vic.' Babe put his arms over his head, crouching into an upright fetal position.* The door pushed open; he felt the cold nose against his cheek. Slowly, stillness returned. Gunner stood by his side underneath the shower spray, one of his most hated experiences, the shower.

Babe stood next to his trusty-furred friend, who shook every inch of his body with fierce movement. The big guy flipped off the water, pulling his towel down to dry his sidekick, who took off. The next thing he heard was Trinity. "Get off the bed! Down, Gunn, down. You're wet, dammit! Vic, where you at?"

Five nights in a row, Babe ran the same routine, and all five had the same result—Nadda. Trinity finally returned to work on Saturday, so his run would be even later, but that was okay. Saturday night meant the college kids would be partying even later. *Perfect.* The one he wanted most of all was the blond-haired guy; the two Latinos were merely his fan club or wannabes. He was the one with the gun. In all fairness, the two probably jumped in once the beating started. No telling, they were all pieces of shit, and did it really matter who gave the deadly blow? No, it didn't. Die, they must, and then Gino.

Babe would end his mission; it was time to retire from the elimination game. He needed to be a dad. They postponed the appointment with her OB because of Chance's death and all that went with it. In another two weeks, they would be back in her office, watching the monitor and seeing their alien child. If the child were a boy, they'd name him Chance; if it was a girl, he wondered if Trinity would consider Astrid or Anna after his grandmother or mother. *A bridge to cross when we get to it.* It was amusing to ponder the nature of their child and who he or she would take after in size since they were opposites; she was tiny, and well, he was anything but.

He and the boys spent the morning working out, then a hot game of HORSE. Babe's basketball skills had improved with very little practice, but the boys were far from slackers. He was as bad as the boys with trash talk. It was fun; since Trinity, he found happiness in many ways. It was unfortunate he couldn't have had childish good times, friends to play with, or a semblance of family, and the crux of it all was Gino. Oddly, he was learning to laugh; she broke the barrier that allowed emotion to flow. His life was what it was, and there was no reason to let it rob him of anymore; he was going to be a dad and a good one. His soul was beginning to feel the serenity of peace, at least at home with Trinity and the boys.

They ate lunch as a family and watched a college football game while Trinity napped with her head in Babe's lap. A few touchdown outbursts temporarily woke her, but he sent her right back to sleep by stroking her hair. Following the game, they went to their bedroom so she could get dressed for work.

Slowly, he stripped her tee shirt over her head. The bra was fitting tighter, and her sleeping shorts slung under her belly, resting on her hips. He kissed her round pudge. She opened the pregnancy app proudly, announcing to him, "We have twenty-two weeks to go; the baby is about five and a half inches from head to rump and weighs five to seven ounces. Right now, we have a cucumber-sized alien or even a chicken breast. Vic, the baby can hiccup. I swear I felt something like that yesterday, but I thought I had gas bubbles." He dropped his jeans, sat on the bed, and pulled her onto his lap, smothering her in soft, sensual kisses.

Turning into the living room, Babe asked, "Anyone want to take the ride to drop off Trinity?" Since Gunner would also be in the vehicle, it would be a tight fit, but he'd make it happen. Chris' phone played some banger sound. The two younger boys goofed around, teasing him because it was Brooke. He shot them the bird and went upstairs. "Chris, tell Trinity we're waiting, and I said to get the lead out."

"Get the lead out?" she responded as she trotted down the stairs. "Really, Vic. I have to look my best; give a girl a minute or two." He watched her. Trinity looked sexy, even pregnant. She had on her stretchy black pants rolled beneath her protruding belly and a black button-up shirt buttoned partially down with a small triangle of her baby bump exposed.

Reg, Jacob, and Gunner climbed in the back seat. Babe held the door open for her and gave her a quick peck. He walked around the car and slid in. She turned the radio to a popular station. The boys instantly started singing the song; Gunner had his nose out the open window. They were like any other family. Babe's breathing was slow and steady, and there wasn't the slightest ripple of tension in his body. Was it the great sex before her work or the joy he found as a family man? *Probably both*, he smiled.

They pulled outside Louie's; Finn strolled out as Trinity slid out the door, followed by faithful Gunn. "Finn, see that she doesn't misbehave." Looking at Trinity, he said, "I'll be here at ten, maybe eleven." She blew him a kiss. They waved, and he took off. He called Ruthie. "Do you want me to pick up something like poboys for dinner, or have you started cooking?" The boys cheered and then pleaded.

She thought for a second, "I suppose poboys would be nice. I'll put tonight's dinner on hold for tomorrow, which means y'all need to eat here and not with her people or prepare to eat both; I'm not letting this chicken go to waste, no sir."

"You got it, ma'am." The boys ragged on him when the call ended. They ribbed him that Ruthie even told him what to do. She was the boss lady. The woman had a heart of gold, and the boys were lucky she took on the role of mom. It was odd how the whole thing came together. For all he knew, he figured Ruthie would move on once his grandfather died. She was a steady hand in his insane world, and it was what the boys needed. He handed Reg the phone and told him to call Parasol's and order six roast beef poboys dressed, the extra one for good measure.

When they pulled up to Parasol's, Babe spotted the blond scuzz-bucket sitting outside alone. He desperately wanted to take care of business, but it wouldn't be appropriate with the boys, and an occasional car passed, not a cool situation. Reg asked if he could go in and pick up the food. "You and Jacob go together." He let the truck idle, walking the boys to the door. The blond asshole didn't recognize him, which was odd, but he did notice his watch. Babe leaned against the hood, pretending to be on the phone. Would the creep walk into trouble or mind his business to live another day? Bending his elbow with the phone at his ear forced his back to the guy. It had to be too tempting for a douche like that to pass up. He palmed a small sharp knife open in his free hand. If and when the person approached demanding the watch, he'd turn and nick his femoral artery enough that it would sting and cause him to flee. He'd make it maybe a block; the bleed-out would take no more than a minute or two. Plan in place, ready to execute if the man was stupid enough.

He didn't bite, so Babe let the opportunity pass, knowing full well if Antoine or anyone from the family knew he didn't act, they'd be pissed, but the opportunity didn't present itself. Besides, he wanted all three thugs.

Moments later, his boys came out of the restaurant, as did the two Mexicans. Reg climbed in and said, "See those two dudes? They're assholes. When they got their order, they inspected it and complained not enough mayo, too much gravy; they were dicks. Ours was ready; we paid and headed out. I'm guessing it was the restaurant manager or something; he told them to take their food and go or leave without the food or a refund. He called them troublemakers. They grabbed their bag, and well, you saw them, they left. If I were a foot taller, I woulda slapped the shit out of them." At least it gave him the info they were uptown. It was a matter of time. They were dead men walking.

While the evening was enjoyable, he was anxious to be with Trinity. He wondered if she'd quit work once the baby came. Would she resent the baby or him for changing her lifestyle? Sometimes, he felt women didn't get a fair shake. Babe was damn glad he wasn't a woman. Markey's face popped into his mind. *Shit, would that have been me as a chick? No fuckin' way.* His thoughts rambled on like an auto-pitch machine. He wouldn't have made a very good woman; he was confident of that.

After eating, the boys went upstairs, and he left. It was about nine-thirty, still early, but he threw caution to the wind and drove around college town. It was refreshingly cool as a breeze buffeted the side of his face. His beard was getting scruffy; he could feel it moving as the draft from open windows ruffled the hair. He stretched his neck, looking at his face in the rearview mirror. Even in the dark, he could see the increased grayness in his beard. *Shit, I'm only thirty-eight and a fucking graybeard.* Nothing he could or would do about that. He knew he had a craggier face than many men his age, but that's what an arid climate caused, and he'd been in the desert a way-long time. Circling onto Pine, he hit the jackpot. All three were standing in the shadows, smoking a reefer; at least it smelled like marijuana. *Perfect.* He continued and then pulled into the first available parking spot. Babe made strides toward them. More interested in getting high, they didn't notice him until he was close enough to grab one. He put one of the Mexicans in a chokehold and flexed, snuffing him. The blond was too wasted to get his gun out fast enough. The compadre of his first kill swung at the big man and tried to kick him. He struck back with his knuckles into the guy's neck. The blond started to run. Babe had him in seconds.

"I got a gun, motherfucker," the guy threatened.

"Do ya now?" The gleam in Babe's eyes was downright demonic. The guy repeated the gun comment. "Then, fuckin' shoot me, you whiny pussy." He could see the guy's hands trembling as he fumbled with the gun. "While you can, you need to run, but I have a parting gift." He slashed up with the small knife, slicing the femoral artery. The blond shrieked and ran. Babe returned to his truck, wiping the blood on a rag in the back seat. He put a lighter to the cloth, and it blazed fiercely. Evidence gone, and murderers eliminated.

Driving toward Louie's, he called Antoine. "Good evening, sir. My apologies for the time, but I wanted you to know mission accomplished."

"Glad to hear it. Thank you, Marine."

Finding a parking spot in the Quarter was exasperating but so worth it when he saw her smile. He'd go to Hell and back for her smile. It said it all; she loved him unquestionably. She poured his two-finger Glenlivet. Since they were no longer dancing on the bar, Shep added bowls of pretzels for the patrons. Babe nibbled on a few, watching her and scanning the place. Everyone was behaving, and it was good times at Louie's.

"Buy you a drink, Marine?" a husky voice asked. He hadn't seen her come in; it was most perplexing, given her size. She nudged closer to the bar.

Babe turned in his seat. It was Markey, and how he could've missed her was mind-blowing. "I already have one, but thanks for the offer." He didn't like her being there; something about the woman was definitely off. He flung a twitch of a smile.

She started with the fifty-question game. No matter how the situation was sliced, even if there wasn't Trinity, Markey was one woman he wouldn't bone; it'd almost be like fucking a guy. *Nope, not for me.* Given his grandmother and mother were tall, sizeable women, perhaps it was why he'd never felt physically attracted to larger framed women. Neither his mother nor grandmother had the slightest touch of masculinity like his co-worker and were considered beautiful women; he still found smaller-boned women more to his liking. Trinity was the quintessential woman of his dreams.

His Creole blossom could tell her man was uncomfortable. Wiping her hands on a towel hanging out of her pocket, she grinned as she approached him. She winked at him and asked Markey what she was drinking. "Whatever he's drinking. Sister girl, this man isn't available; try someone else." Babe became intrigued by the interaction. Would she go all territorial or politely respond or ignore the woman?

"Glenlivet it is." She winked at Markey. "Yep, this guy is one hundred percent taken," she said, holding up her left hand. She had changed from diamonds to her pink band. Babe chuckled loudly.

"Markey, meet my wife, Trinity. My girl," thumbing toward his peculiar co-worker, "this is the mason and welder I told you about." He had totally forgotten to mention it to her before. Trinity played along, saying it was nice to meet her and put a face to the name. "You staying til twelve, or you wanna bug out earlier?" She said she was ready, rubbing her belly. He drained his drink, patted Markey on the shoulder, and said, "See you in the morning, ma'am." Trinity spoke briefly with Finn as Babe walked to the far end of the bar, where he greeted her with a kiss, took her hand, and they walked out.

On the way to the truck, he told her about the first time he met Markey. While shocked by the boldness of his co-worker, she laughed, saying it was obvious the woman had a crush on him.

When they got to the truck, he helped her inside, circled the front, and slid in, cranking the engine. "I don't know how to put this, but I've made Chance's murderers pay. Before you ask, yes, your dad knows. Because we are married, in a court of law, an attorney cannot ask you to confirm or deny a charge brought against me. It's called spousal privilege. It won't come to that, but to relieve any stress you may have, I wanted you to know you are protected. When's the next doctor's appointment?"

With Gunner at the ready, prancing and barking, the world knew Babe and Trinity were home. "Shh, Gunn, you could wake the dead," she instructed the dog. There were a few rumbles from the other bedrooms.

Babe watched as she peeled her clothes off. Her expressions were comical. He turned on the shower, "Get that funk-nasty off you," he chuffed. She laughed at him, mimicking her. Twisting her hair up and clipping it, they entered the shower together. He lathered a sponge up and washed her body. Trinity took the sponge from him and started scrubbing him. "Girl, look what you've done to me." She squealed that she hadn't even come close to Mr. Happy. He lifted her, stepped out of the shower, and wrapped them in a jumbo bath sheet.

WORTH THE TIME

*A*ppointment day was upon them. Trinity bubbled on and on, predicting the baby was a boy, convinced he'd look like Babe. She asked what he thought. *Hmm. What do I think?* Was he hoping for a boy? Having a girl would be a challenge; he knew nothing about girls, and what he did know wasn't for mixed company. Anna Marie was the name chosen for a girl, and Chance B. for a boy. Babe put his foot down about using his name but acquiesced for an initial. His official name would be Chance B. Vicarelli—no middle name. In his opinion, they should give the baby Trinity's last name. It would certainly open more doors.

Hand in hand, they walked into Dr. Monroe's office. The same routine he suspected of all moms-to-be: pee in a cup, get on the scale, strip off the clothes, get in a gown, and feet in the stirrups. No twat invasion during this visit, only hooking up to the monitor. The baby's heartbeat bounced off the walls. The doctor said everything sounded good with the baby. This time, the image was a perfect baby, no more alien look-alike. "Just making sure; y'all want to know before we proceed. The rascal is in a tight ball and isn't revealing anything, but give your little one a minute, and I'm sure we'll get a view." Yes, they wanted to know. The baby moved enough to see her in all her glory.

"A girl, what?" Trinity exclaimed. "A girl." Her eyes teared up. *Happy or upset?* Babe was confused. "Do you think we can name a girl Chance?" *Herein lies the issue*, he determined. "I know I told you we could use your mom's name, but—"

His smile was the broadest she'd ever seen. "Wow, a girl. Of course, her name can be Chance, maybe Chance Marie? My girl, we have plenty of time to decide, but it's whatever you want. You're doing all the heavy lifting on this; I'm the recipient of your hard work." Like before, they had several pictures. When measuring the baby, Dr. Monroe mentioned the development was perfect, and the baby was a good size. They were going to monitor it closely. When asked, Babe had no idea how much he weighed when he was born. No, he wasn't aware of any baby books, and there was no one he could ask. Gino wouldn't know, and whatever the fucker said would be a lie. Maybe Mays might know how big he was, and then they could estimate Babe's approximate weight.

Trinity and Doctor Monroe were chattering away as his mind rolled through the kaleidoscope of thoughts. He'd always been a big kid, and Gino was six feet, just an inch taller than his mother, which, as he remembered, was a sticking point with them. *Need to finish the business with Gino.*

Trinity cut one of the pictures for him to show Glenn, who was more anxious to have a baby than her sister. Bethany had never mentioned wanting kids, ever, in all the time growing up, whereas Trinity dreamt about a family like her parents with tons of kids. Growing up with five brothers and a sister was the best. He parked at the hotel, walked her to the apartment, and took off on foot to the Conti Street job.

Glenn was having a heated discussion with Markey when Babe arrived. She looked like she was about to deck him. He didn't feel comfortable walking into their dispute but didn't want it to escalate. In a jovial tone, he called over to Glenn, "We have pictures, Boss," providing the ideal getaway from Markey. Friendly was not his nature, certainly not acting all cheesedick, but it served its purpose. *Who sounds like a motherfucking pussy, now?* He berated himself.

Babe handed him the ultrasound image. "And? I don't see any junk.

Man, a girl, aww, she's gonna break your heart and have you wrapped around her little finger. I see how you are with spoiled Miss Trinity, sucka!" They both got a chuckle out of the comment. *Too true*, he thought. His little woman definitely controlled the strings as though he were a marionette.

He usually wasn't one for gossip and didn't give a hearty shit about other people's business, but things looked intense with Markey, so he asked Glenn. The crux was that he had to ensure proper protocol and maintain a working atmosphere as site super. He didn't micromanage the day-to-day teasing or crude remarks, but a couple of the men had complained about her constant sexual pressing. It had to be off-the-charts obnoxious if they were disturbed by it and annoyed, knowing his crew. They could be a rough group. When confronted, Markey became defensive, according to Glenn.

Putting on the hard hat, Babe cautioned, "The chick is fuckin' nuts, chief. She has said some off-the-wall things to me and then showed up at Louie's. Bordering on stalking. Be on guard. I've never hit a woman, but my opinion might change if she goes after you." Those were his parting words heading to the area of construction. He avoided Markey.

The forklift beeped as it backed into position, lowering a palette of bricks. Cinder block exterior walls defined the footprint of the building. As the interior projects of wiring, plumbing, and ductwork came into play, the brick masons were ready to start working on the exterior. The site was a rumble of noise from machinery, instruction shouts, and blaring music. It was the interior of the building that would require a significant amount of time with all its finery and old-world details. Schlepping plywood sheets was a brainless function requiring brute strength and endurance, which he had in spades, opening his mind to thoughts of Gino.

When would be an opportune moment to do the deed? First, he would have questions. He'd already waited more than his patience would allow. If the sperm donor was still a creature of habit, Babe remembered Gino would waltz to Liuzza's with a self-important swagger. He'd slick his hair back with some greasy pomade, laden himself with too much cologne, and wear a heavy gold chain bearing a religious medal; saintly soul he was, ha! Then it dawned on him: *yes, Trinity, I am Catholic, never went to church or partook in the religious rites of passage.*

His first plan required the stealth of night and silently waiting for him to come home. Looking at a different option, maybe more menacing, would be to brazenly knock on his door and watch the horror come to the man's face. He'd begin the conversation with the usual discourse, catching up, per se. Babe would grill him on Mays, making sure to mention they had met. Once he could see Gino's guard was down, he'd walk behind him with a pretense of getting water or the like and do the deed, commenting about Mays' hearing loss. *Fucking bastard beat him to deafness. Yeah, he'll pay, alright.*

Thinking of Mays brought warmth to his heart. Trinity called him a giant teddy bear. He was a kind, gentle soul. Babe laughed out loud, thinking about when Mays took charge. Lissa was blown away. He had obviously pampered and provided a life for her beyond her wildest dreams, and yet, the bitch treated him like shit. Babe wondered if the trend started on their visit persisted or if his brother went back to his natural happy-go-lucky persona. Part of him hoped the warrior side remained, while another part wanted him to be himself and not feel like he needed to live up to anyone but his own standards.

Glenn's whistle pierced the commotion of the construction site. "Lunch truck," he called out. The workers lined up or took their lunch pales and sat away from the fray of the food truck. The offerings were slim pickings: hamburger, ham and cheese sandwich, hot dog with chili, and fish sandwich. Two blocks over was a hole in the wall with lunch specials. He informed Glenn and hoofed it for baked chicken and macaroni, with a salad comprised of four pieces of iceberg lettuce and a drizzle of ranch dressing. The dry chicken and almost crunchy mac indicated they had been under the heat lamp too long, but their banana pudding was excellent. He swigged down two bottles of water. What he desired was a big plate of spaghetti and meatballs with a sizeable piece of Italian bread.

Walking to the site, he called Ruthie. "Everything okay, honey?"

"Yes, ma'am. Can I put in a request for dinner?" It was his house, and she worked for him; of course, he could, but he didn't play the game that way.

"What you hankering for?" Her voice emitted a sound of mirth. The man had never asked for specific dinners; there was always a first.

"Meatballs and spaghetti. Is it a problem?"

"Smart minds think alike. I already have a tasty red gravy simmering on the stove. Now, I don't wanna give our expectant mother heartburn, so I added a little sugar, and that should cut down on the acid, but if she needs me to fix something special for her—"

"No, ma'am, she'll be at Louie's. Shep will make sure our girl eats. Thanks, look forward to dinner."

Back to planning the Gino execution, he tossed different scenarios at the wall to see what stuck. Given his truck, broad daylight would be risky, but if he used the sedan, it wouldn't garner as much attention; besides, he'd park down the block. *Yeah, confrontation was the ticket. Let the bastard sweat a little.*

Once on-site, he returned to moving cumbersome objects like the plywood. His mind hadn't checked out yet with the mundane, and it was a good thing because he saw the forklift begin to tip. The mass of workers saw it simultaneously and ran to help. If the palette of brick had hit the ground, it would have crumbled to pieces and been a significant cost. Babe shoved an iron fire container for scraps as a brace, and then he and five others pushed against the lean. Markey moved one of the men and got on the opposite end from Babe. There was no doubt he felt when she added her force. The bitch was as strong or stronger than most of the men on the site. The forklift lowered the palette, unloaded its haul, and everyone could breathe again. *Disaster averted.*

"Markey," Babe called out. She pivoted in his direction. "Impressive, ma'am." She smiled and curled her guns. Was that a break in her awkwardness, *maybe?* Or, on the other hand, did it open the door for her to solicit uninvited gestures? There was no doubt the woman wasn't playing with a full deck.

Work returned to brainless tasking, giving him time to savor the vision of Gino wildly animated, trying to pull off the man of importance charade he always pursued, at least to Babe's recollection. Gino's perception of himself was a story of delusion, always had and always would be, until the final curtain. Why was it that men, maybe people, of such insecurity had to mask in an ideology of a big-shot? Gino's take was that the higher the rung on the ladder of the world, the more he could demand people around him to perform useless tasks for the sake of feeling superior. The truth was simple: the higher the position, the greater the responsibility and the vastly increased workload and pressure. It was much easier having someone command instruction, plotting the plan and execution while assuming full responsibility for a successful outcome.

While he had risen in the military ranks, he looked at it more as duty than an ego stroke. He was responsible for the safety of his team, and on the missions where he lost some, the blame, he felt, fell on him. He'd let them down. It was serious business. He would have gladly changed places with any of the Marines he lost.

So entrenched in his thoughts, the stacks of plywood sheets had dwindled to nothing with the spinning of his mind. Glenn called Babe into the office. "Is Trinity still working Tuesday through Saturday?" Babe tipped his head in curiosity but confirmed. "Jeez, when is she gonna give it up?" The big man put his hands up in surrender, saying it wasn't his place and the family knew how obstinate she could be, so whoever wanted to challenge her was welcomed, but they'd already had the conversation, and she'd basically told him to fuck off. Babe trusted her enough to know she'd call it quits if she suspected it was causing an issue with the pregnancy. Just given her response to the bout of cramping she'd had as the ligaments stretched was a clear indication of how protective she was with the pregnancy.

Quitting time came faster than he realized, as usual. He jogged to Louie's. Whatever the case was with the blender, she was at it again. Her sweet smile warmed him like a shearling blanket. He sat for a moment while she fiddled with the appliance, muttering a string of obscenities under her breath. He used the time to call Ruthie. "How's dinner coming? I'm gonna be a bit late; please make my plate and set it in the microwave. I don't want to mess up the household schedule, ma'am."

Trinity walked around the bar and sat on the stool next to him. "Shep needs to buy a few more blenders. These are probably the first ones ever made. Fixing them is a pain in my ass, and no one else takes the responsibility, not even Finn. When he sees me almost finished, he'll say, 'Oh, let me do that.' I tell him he's a little late to rescue the damsel," and she laughed. "Nah, he's awesome. You gonna be late tonight; what cha got goin'?" She cranked the blender up, and it sounded like it was crushing nails. He hardly thought it sounded fixed.

Arms around his neck, she stood on the footrail of the bar and zeroed in for a kiss. It was a perfect move, letting him off the hook, hence avoiding the answer. He hated lying to her but didn't feel comfortable saying, I'm on my way to kill my father. He kissed her again, said he'd see her at ten or eleven, and bolted. Still consumed by the blender, she mumbled something like she'd see him then.

The guy from the garage had his truck parked for an easy exit. Driving down Canal Street, he checked the glove box where he kept a screwdriver, pliers, flashlight, flares, and lighter. He placed the screwdriver on the console. Traffic on Canal moved quickly, everyone wanting to get home from work, landing him a block from Gino's lickety-split. He put the tool in his pocket. With bold, determined steps, he reached the front door and knocked. Babe could hear shuffling and grumbles. The door swung open. Separated by a screen door, his father looked at the massive man on his porch. There was a slight indication of recognition, yet he was unsure. "Yeh, what can I do for you?" The voice he knew so well bore into his spine like an electric screw gun and bit into plywood sheets.

He couldn't say, father or dad, so he left it at "I'm Babe."

The man took a step back, fear written all over his face. "I thought it was you." Keeping Babe on the porch.

Forcing a smile, he said, "I'm in New Orleans, my time with the Corps served, and I wanted to stop by." He was still on the porch, wondering if he would have to power his way through. Gino squinted his eyes, studying everything about the man on his porch. "I have questions that only you can answer. My wife, a tiny woman, is pregnant, and given our remarkable difference in size, her doctor asked how much I weighed as a baby, and I don't know, so thought I'd see if you remembered."

Finally, Gino pushed open the screen door. "I guess she shocked you with that—damn women, making these decisions on their own. Now you gonna have to support the kid and your wife. Hmmpf." He turned and started to walk into the house. "Let's take a seat in the kitchen. Sorry, I only have three chairs; oh yeah, you'd know that." Babe thought *slimy piece of shit*. Gino was building even more of a case for his extermination. *Heartless*. Maybe if he'd seemed the least bit regretful, it might make the deed more difficult, but he was the same cunt he'd been when Babe was a boy, just older with deep crevices of substance abuse and hard living etched on his face. The older man sat with a lit cigarette in the ashtray and an open beer. "I have to say, you look the part of a Marine. You ever see any fighting?" He asked sarcastically.

"Yes, I was special ops, a Raider, several tours, and way too many missions: Afghanistan, Iraq, Africa, and other countries filled with hate and strife. Before I forget, how much did I weigh at birth?" Babe sat with his hands folded on the table, managing his anger.

Gino drew a lungful of smoke, the tip of his cigarette glowing orange with smoke enveloping his head. He coughed a few times. The man looked sick, probably riddled with cancer; he had a grey wash to his complexion. Maybe let the devil take him with pain and torment as his body gave way to disease. No, Babe had a plan, a good one, and it paid the bastard back for the damage he caused Mays. "You were nine pounds plus, if I remember right. You could have been eight or ten pounds, but I think nine. You know what it's like fucking someone that had a big ass baby pass through there?" Babe bit his tongue; he wanted nothing more than to pound him until he was nothing but pulp. *Not yet.* "Make her get a Cesarean is my advice. That way, everything stays like it should." *What a narcissistic bastard.*

The two men had no similarities besides their dark hair and olive complexion. Their faces were completely different. Babe had a more chiseled structure to his face, like his grandfather. The sperm donor had a narrow face with undiscernible cheekbones, a hooked nose, and a pointy chin. Gino's build leaned on the side of scrawny, yet when Babe was a boy, the man seemed so robust, but that was from a kid's perspective. Ruthie was right; Babe looked like his grandfather, only with a different coloring. For his entire adult life, he had pictured Gino with his face, but it was a nightmare he'd created. He knew from being around his grandfather their resemblance was striking. The little house brought back horrifying memories. They rolled through his mind like an old-time movie reel. He wondered what ghosts haunted his old man. Did he remember the pain his twelve-year-old son inflicted upon him? How degrading it had to have been. *Good. It was worth every damn therapy session.*

"I met Mays, by the way," Babe said tauntingly. "He's a prominent attorney in Atlanta. He looks just like our mother." Babe had a smug sound to his voice, and he knew it; no matter how hard he tried to be non-confrontational, it wasn't working.

The wide-eyed expression on Gino's face screamed shock. Babe was never to find out, and he did. *Fuck you.* The man cleared his throat and seemed shaky. "Rune promised your mother he'd never tell you. Such a liar. Always was an asshole." Babe moved his hands from the table to his thighs, holding control. Gino guzzled the beer.

Babe looked him in the eyes, "He didn't tell me; he kept the promise. After he died, I called his brother, Bjorn, in Narvik. While it was mid-morning here, it was after the drinking hour there, and he'd had a snootful. I asked if any other relatives might want some of my grandfather's possessions. He said no but slipped, saying, 'Maybe your—' and stopped there. I pressed the issue, and he said what the hell and told me. Mays is a great guy; we've become close. We may even take a trip to Narvik together. I haven't seen Bjorn since I was a kid, and Mays has never met him."

Gino lit another cigarette, smoke filling the tiny kitchen. He began choking from his inhalation, so Babe got up to fill a glass of water for the old man, but his purpose was far from helping. "Unfortunately, Mays is deaf in one ear and has hearing loss in the other. Do you know why?" He stood behind the chair with his screwdriver in his hand and leaned toward the old man's ear, "Because you motherfucker smacked him around so much as a tiny child. Fuck you." He drove the screwdriver into the man's ear, twisting it to inflict the maximum damage possible and breach his brain. Death wasn't instantaneous, so there was suffering, but not enough to fill his thirst for torture, to Babe's dismay. Gino slumped onto the table with the lit cigarette still wedged between his nicotine-stained fingers. After ten minutes of wiping down anything he may have touched, he left the house, avoiding contact with anything on the way out. As soon as he got in the truck, he called Mays and drove off.

On the third ring, he picked up. "No way, I was just talking about you to the kids. Man, so sorry you didn't get to meet my parents. How'd things go with Trinity's brother?" It was good to hear his voice. As before, he had a genuine, welcoming tone.

"Trinity's brother, Chance, died, sorry to say."

"Oh my God. Poor little thing. I'll pray for her and her family. I keep you in my prayers always, brother." He paused momentarily. "How? That doesn't matter; there's no need to bring up sad feelings. It's just good to hear from you. Have your passports come in yet?"

"No, not yet." He inhaled deeply, "My girl is a wreck; it's no wonder. Her family is super tight, and they were like, what's the saying? The one that comes to mind is my right hand and my dick, but maybe red beans and rice sounds nicer. Anyway, you'll meet them all one day when you come to New Orleans to see me. The reason I called, you can't say anything to anyone, got it?" Mays confirmed. "Gino will no longer be a problem to anyone, ever." Silence. "You there?" He had about ten minutes until he was home, and the phone call had to end before then.

"Hang on, I'm moving into the study." Babe could hear him walking across the house. He remembered the rooms and what they looked like, figuring the study door would close any minute. "Fuck, Babe, what happened?"

He put his blinker on to turn; he'd pull up in the driveway in minutes. "I told you I was going to do it. I don't threaten; I do. He needed to pay for what he did to you."

The gasp echoed in Babe's ear. "Jesus, how'd you do it?" His curiosity was almost voyeuristic. He wanted description, every detail, and was full of questions. "I probably should feel sad, but I don't. Part of me wishes I had helped you." He changed the subject. "Are you still planning on Narvik?"

"Absolutely, once the fucking passports come. Look, I'm pulling into the driveway, and the call will get noisy. I'll call you as soon as we get them."

Mays interjected. "It'll only be three of us. Lissa isn't going; that's a story for another time."

"I'll call you back when I get inside and settled. An hour work?" Babe responded, hoping it wasn't his influence. Had he squeezed the toothpaste out of the tube?

Mays affirmed an hour was fine.

The aroma of garlic bread filled the air like an Italian bistro. Ruthie had everything ready for him. "Ma'am, it sure smells good." Reg and Jacob were at the table finishing a piece of chocolate cake. "Where's Chris?"

Both boys rolled their eyes, "He's on the phone with Amanda and has been in the bathroom for a long time."

Babe took a bite of the spaghetti and meatballs, and unlike the four pieces of lettuce from the hole-in-the-wall eatery close to work, Ruthie's salad cascaded from the plate it was heaping. He ate quietly, thinking about Mays and Lissa. It wasn't a match made in heaven, that was for sure, but he didn't pick up on separation. Babe laughed to himself; Trinity's comment about men's lack of observation filled his head. Thinking back, how could he have missed the signs of pregnancy; he thought she looked healthy and not waif-like. Recounting Mays and Lissa's interaction and her condescending manner toward his brother started to paint a different picture than he initially conjured.

"What, no comment about him being that long in the bathroom on the phone with Amanda?" Reg teased.

Babe looked up, his eyebrows furrowed together, "Wait, Amanda? What about Brooke?"

Jacob spoke up, "Ancient history, big man. The hows and whys of the break up is an unspoken issue." They both started to laugh. The daily drama of teenagers wasn't something he needed to concern himself with as long as everyone was okay.

He took a few more bites of the salad. "He's okay?"

Jacob grabbed Reg's plate and brought them into the kitchen, leaving Reg to answer. "Oh, he's fine; so's she." He held cupped hands at his chest, indicating the new girlfriend was well-endowed.

Babe waited for Jacob to return to the dining room. "Y'all remember the conversation about respect and how to treat girls?" He understood the fascination but hoped they weren't acting like jackasses.

Pressing in his mind was getting back to Mays. "Y'all need to shut that shit down when Ruthie's in listening distance. Understand, or do I need to spell it out?" They acknowledged his comment. Chris entered the dining room, sweat dripping off his face. "Just get out of the shower?" Babe asked. The other two broke into laughter. Chris struck back with a glare and a hidden flick-off.

Plates empty, he returned the dishes to the kitchen, where he learned the inside scoop about Chris and Brooke from Ruthie and how this new Amanda-girl was not from the sort of people she thought Chris should associate with. Pictures of Gino flashed through his mind; he knew precisely the kind of family Ruthie referenced. His trials and tribulations growing up made him iffy advising young boys about dating protocol. He hadn't the first clue. They were good kids, dealt a crappy hand, and he had improved their lives. Ruthie was more than up to the task of guiding them.

After dinner, he moved to the formal living room. Ruthie was bound to shoot him scolding looks. The formal living room was for show, he guessed. Mays answered on the first ring. "That was quick. Brother, there's not much to tell. You know Lissa was an arranged marriage—"

Babe cut him off, "Mail order bride?"

"Right. Da Nang, actually a village or town just outside, was rough for girls; the men often abused them, especially beautiful young ladies. Anyway, her parents sold her and her sister for survival. Lissa's name was Lien, which I thought was beautiful, but she wanted an American name and picked Lissa. She no more wanted to marry me than fly to the moon, but when she saw I had money, there was a sudden interest. She tolerated the pregnancies but had little time for our kids. I saw it from the onset and hired an au pair. Gretchen became part of the family and was with us until last year. They usually only stay for a set time, but we paid the company all the expenses out of pocket, and she stayed with us. She wanted to attend college in the States, so I paid for her college, and she helps out sometimes with carpooling." Babe listened but didn't need the dissertation. He wanted the facts, plain and simple. "The bottom line is that Lissa wanted out of the American family life and asked for a divorce. Oh, and a settlement." He coughed out a chuckle. "She'll find herself another rich man without children. The kids and I are okay."

The concept of abandoning her children was something Babe found puzzling. Perhaps, a year or two previously, he wouldn't have given any thought to the idea and accepted it as, 'whatever.' Trinity created splendid avenues he'd never crossed—love, family, playfulness, and a want for togetherness. Even though their baby was still growing inside her, Babe loved his little one with all his heart. *A girl, well, God really does have a sense of humor.* The God Entity had started becoming his reality. *How's that grab you, Trey?*

BAD NEWS

*G*lenn knew they were waiting on passports for a two-week Norwegian holiday. Day by day, their routine stayed the same. It was the mere passing of time, and having a rhythm without any big shakes felt good. It had been four weeks since Gino's demise. The NOPD hadn't knocked on his door, so as far as he knew, no one complained of his father's absence or questioned his death. It was a sad state of affairs; the man hadn't left a legacy of any sort—no friends, no family, no one who gave a damn—*Poof, like dust in the wind.*

Trinity and Finn's routine behind the bar had settled, and while the crowd still came to see them, she wasn't shaking it as much. Juggling the bottle back and forth amused new onlookers.

Sipping his Glenlivet, he watched sizing up the guests as they entered. It had been a while since he'd seen Max or Trey, so he was surprised when the two entered. They moved straight to him. Max was the first to speak. "So you got that sweet Creole lady to marry you, and I can see she's baking your bun. Congratulations, bro. Girl or boy?"

Babe beamed, "Girl," and looked at Trinity.

Trey proudly flashed a few new pictures of his baby, Presley Jane. The detectives said they'd come from a crime scene on Conti, which perked Babe's ears. Neighbors called in the body of a dead man in a doorway; it was the second in two days. "It was down a block from your father-in-law's construction site," Trey remarked. "I'm sure it'll be the buzz at work tomorrow. By the way, remember the three guys that you and ya friend detained? They got their comeuppance uptown near Broadway." Babe muttered like he wasn't surprised; if looking for trouble, people usually found it. "You got any family in the area?"

"No, all my family died. The last one to go was my grandfather, my mother's father." He gazed with softness at Trinity, "And now, the one on the way." He returned his attention to Trey.

"I asked because I heard through a friend from Mid-City about a gruesome crime scene, and the vic's name was Vicarelli. You're the only one I know with that last name. If he's kin, I thought you might want to know."

"My sperm donor was a Vicarelli. He abused the shit out of my mother, and when I was twelve, I broke his shoulder, where he could no longer hit anyone. Man, they had me on a shrink's couch for years, but the police didn't arrest him, the bastard. After that, my mother and I moved in with her parents. I don't know what ever happened to the motherfucker. I doubt he made it this long. He was an alcoholic and a mean drunk at that. No way he'd still be kickin'. If it was him, I sure as shit wouldn't shed any tears."

They observed as he watched Trinity. The Marine had softened a little since meeting him the first time and was not quite as on edge. The girl had worked miracles. After hearing about Babe's father, he could see where the big man might have developed his acute awareness and standoffishness.

Trey couldn't imagine having an abusive father. Sure, he got the belt a time or two, but it's because he was mouthy and deserved it. His family was no different than the other families in the neighborhood. He could imagine what would've happened to any kids threatening to call child protection. The worst parent, as far as quick to the belt, lived two doors down; they could hear the dad yelling, 'You gonna cry, then I'm gonna give you something to cry about.' Trey's mom would give the eye to his dad and shake her head. His parents disapproved, but back then, nobody would say a dang thing about how a person raised or punished their child. Now, the world was overladen with disrespectful, puddin' kids that would threaten their parents with the likes of child protective services. Nope, not in his house; it was a new, different generation and not for the better—spoiled, whiny, spineless turds who felt entitled.

They caught the wink between Babe and Trinity. He checked the time. "My girl has new hours. She gets off at twelve, but sometimes eleven. Bold changes are happening in our lives; as you say, Trey, God is Good." The detective nodded and said he was happy to hear those words from Babe's mouth.

The three men jawed for the next thirty minutes. The detectives probably told him more than they should about the two murders in two days. The victims were male and had gotten the snot beat out of them; they said it looked like a knee plant to the face—flattened noses, broken teeth, but definite punches to the cheekbones and sides of the head. The medical examiner would determine the cause of death, but more than likely, internal organ damage. *So, New Orleans has another serial killer, not my beef.* He saw her grab her backpack and knew it was time to leave. She looked tired, and he was ready to put her to bed.

It was downright cold on his morning run. The sun was beginning to peek into the horizon, but with the massive live oak trees, the canopy of their branches made the already cold conditions even more biting. He started pondering the dilemma of their passports. They should be arriving any day; time was of the essence. Hopefully, they'd come in soon. From the way it looked, they might be traveling between Thanksgiving and Christmas, having to be home for both holidays. The beginning of December would be preferable, but it was going to be colder than any temperature his wife had experienced. Norway in December, he figured, was fucking insane. Once home and in his room, he stripped and got into a steamy shower. The job site was going to be cold. The city was generally windier, cutting through to the bone.

Trinity stayed in her pajamas, stuffed her backpack with jeans and work clothes, slung it over her shoulder, and was ready to go. He knew what she'd do, climb from the bed at home to the one at the apartment. Leaving her tucked in bed was nearly impossible. He wanted to climb in next to her and love her passionately, but he'd have to put those thoughts on hold for the time being.

The wind whipped through the old buildings, making the narrow streets like wind tunnels. Glenn had the trailer warm; one or two people would periodically take their break in the office with a cup of joe. It was cold, but not the icy conditions he'd fought in. Markey seemed to brave the unusual coldness as Babe did, never once breaking for the warmth of Glenn's trailer. It was more than apparent many of the men would skirt a wide girth from the woman. She stayed to herself; her work was balls-on-accurate, and she'd displayed a team player mentality more than once. It perplexed him why she was ostracized. Because she was a woman? Was it the inappropriate comments she'd made? If so, they needed to man up and get the fuck over it. Or was there something else? She was certifiably crazy; he knew that from their first encounter.

Babe assessed her. She was a tall, built woman with more muscle than most of the men on site. Was that it? Did she intimidate them? Her face was attractive in an angular way, too masculine for him, but it wasn't like she was butt-ugly. Besides, he thought, he'd seen some of the nasty skirts some of the men were drilling, and Markey was far better than the likes of them. It might be a different scenario in tight jeans or without a toolbelt hanging from her hips and wearing a hard hat. The night she showed up at Louie's, he'd been annoyed, so he never really sized up her appearance. Why did he even give two shits—Trinity was wearing off on him.

The lunch truck pulled up with two additional items added to their menu. The new offerings were taco soup and a Philly cheesesteak sandwich;

neither appealed to him. He joined the queue, observing who got what. One thing for sure, he wasn't trying the taco soup; it looked like watered-down ketchup, with a few chunks of ground beef or cat, tortilla strips, and a blob of sour cream and cheese. *Flying shits*. Their hamburgers were decent and safe. From over his shoulder, Markey said, "Not adventurous, Vicarelli? No taco soup for you? I bet it's enough to clean your system out," she laughed.

"No, sure and steady, hamburger." A gust blew down Conti, almost everyone punctuating the blast with some profanity. Babe cupped his hands, put them to his mouth, and blew, trying to keep them warm and not letting a stiffness move in with the iciness.

"Here, take one of these. Fur-lined, yet can take a beating." He glanced at her exposed hand, declining the glove, a word about the fit. She was big, but his hands were too big for her glove. Her knuckles were bruised and scraped. If it were a guy, he'd bet odds they'd been in a knockdown, ass-kicking. She saw him take note and casually said, "You shoulda seen the other guy," and chuckled. The hairs on his arms prickled; there was something about her comment that had authenticity, not just cliché candor.

"I bet," he nodded, tilting his head. Trey's description of the dead men resonated in the back of his mind. *Fuck, it's her; I know it. What do they say it takes one to know one? No proof, just gut.* Maybe the other guys knew and kept their distance. His order was up just in time. He was beginning to feel awkward. Gino was going to be his last; he'd made that decision. His inner voice said, walk away; it is not yours to do. He nodded as he passed her. *Do not engage.*

Five o'clock rolled around; he was anxious to leave. He stopped in at Louie's; Trinity's back was to him. She was looking down at whatever was in her hand. "Don't tell me, fucking blender again?"

She turned, "Isn't this the most precious thing?" She had a kitten snuggled in her hands. He was mostly white with what looked like a black mustache and heavy black eyebrows. His tiny paws looked to have black socks, and then, as the icing on the cake, half his tail was black and the other white as if he'd dipped it in a paint bucket. Babe put his hand out, and the tiny kitten didn't even fill his hand. "Isn't he adorbs? I think I'll name him either Groucho or Toulouse."

"He's a cute little fella, for sure, and I get the Groucho, but Toulouse?" He stroked his tiny back.

"He's so tiny, and Toulouse-Lautrec was small. He had some affliction. Besides, it's so N'awlins." She longingly looked into Babe's eyes—her smile, sweet and loving.

Gunner was already circling his legs, looking at the object in his hands. Babe stooped down. "Gunner, meet your new friend, Groucho." Looking up at Trinity, his eyes twinkled; he'd made her sparkle with excitement. "No cat in our bed. We'll get him a bed of his own. Ruthie is gonna have a fucking stroke. If this little motherfucker starts marking his territory, he's out the door. We need to get him chopped as soon as possible. The litter box goes outside when he's big enough to go through a cat door. Fuck me. Girl, you have me wrapped around your little finger. What the hell is gonna happen to me when I have two of y'all? I need a drink." He sat, holding the kitten in one hand.

Babe soon left for the house with their newly acquired family member. Running like a faucet were images of Markey. What would have caused her to beat someone to death? Had they attacked her first, and it was self-defense? Somehow, it didn't smack of that and was more like cold-calculated murder. He had established she was crazy, and maybe she had some underlying thing about men. Did she want to be a man? She had said she liked dick, so maybe not. Did she want a man desperately enough that when it didn't work out, she killed them? There were plenty of men out there that liked Amazonian women. Would she be prowling for the next victim that night? Something had to have ignited the killer in her to reveal itself. What was the spark?

Pulling up to Chestnut, Chris met him at the truck. "When can I take driver's ed? Please sign off on it because it's due tomorrow with a check for two hundred and fifty dollars. I know it's a lot, but please." Babe hadn't even had time to get out of the truck. He opened the door, reaching for the new tiny package. Suddenly, Chris' attention was on the kitten. "Where'd the cat come from?"

"Trinity." They walked into the house. "Chris, let me settle, go through the mail, talk with Ruthie, and then I'll sign the permission slip and cut a check for two fifty. Take a breath, little dude." As suspected, Ruthie took one look at the kitten, remarking kittens were cute, but cats were destructive. What was he thinking bringing a cat into the house? Lifting the tail, she gasped about it being a male. "Maybe it'll be a Louie's cat? Kitten here, cat at Louie's." She huffed for a second, putting her arms out to cuddle the kitten. "His name is Groucho, per Trinity."

"Between you and your wife, this place is becoming a menagerie. It went from one impeccable gentleman to a man with the vocabulary of a sailor; don't think I don't hear." He corrected, saying he was a Marine. "Yes, Marine, sorry, it's still the Navy." She rolled her eyes. "Now a man, woman, child on the way, three orphaned boys, a dog, and now a cat. Mister Rune must be rolling in his grave. Sir, please do not bring any more animals into this house." She had a way of standing with her back straight as a board and an air of command. *Yep, she would've made a fine Marine.*

Reg and Jacob were down the street and would be back before dark, which was momentarily, and he'd be able to spend time with them. The kitten was the hit of the evening. Babe signed all the papers and wrote the check for driver's education, which prompted Chris to start talking about cars. He watched as Reg and Jacob held onto his every word. It amazed him how the boys fell into their roles so quickly. Chris had the authority and panache of the oldest. Reg was the middle child, full of character to glean attention, and Jacob played the role of youngest well, with complete adoration of Chris and competing for attention with Reg.

Babe found a stick in the backyard and tied a string to it with a clothespin on the end. He showed the boys how to entertain the cat, trailing the clothespin along the floor and teasing the cat so he would chase it. They laughed as Groucho, springing from all four legs to the side, a typical kitten move, chased the string. Their entertainment carried on for most of the evening. Babe's phone buzzed. "Vicarelli."

It was Daniel. "Captain, it's Collins. I haven't heard from you in a while and was checking to see if everything was cool. I know you and the Commander were tight." *If you only knew ol' Danny boy.* "If you're free one night, maybe we could get a drink." He hemmed and hawed, "Um, your girl ever come up with an idea of a single friend?" If it was sex he wanted, Samantha came to mind; she was as easy as they came, and he figured Daniel would think she was hot. Bursting through was Markey's face. *Oh, hell no.* She wanted a man alright, but had the two victims insulted her, and that's why she killed them, or was it a thing after sex, instead of a smoke or pillow talk? Did she do the deeds? *Who knows?* He had let the speculation morph into fact. It was a gut feeling; there was nothing factual about his hypotheses.

"I'll be heading to Louie's between ten and eleven; my girl gets off at midnight." They agreed to meet again for a drink. Call finished; he turned on the television in time to see the latest breaking news: Hammas had slaughtered a crowd of people at a concert. "Fucking hell!"

He heard Ruthie clear her throat.

"Ruthie, you need to see this." She entered, dropping her jaw as she read the scrolling bottom of the screen.

"Lawd, have mercy." She looked at Babe in question, "You think we're on the brink of World War III?" She watched, wringing her hands, and sat on the edge of a wing-back chair, "What does this mean? We already mixed up with the Ukraine war."

His eyes squared off as he watched the news unfold, and it wasn't looking good. It was a known fact no one should fuck with the Israelis. Would this bring the United States to fight alongside Israel? It damn well should. Opinions of America's weakness ran rampant, and what once was the most powerful nation in the world had slowly turned, making them a laughing stock. Those in control totally fucked up Afghanistan, and he'd witnessed it for himself. He was there and questioned why orders were to move out. He wanted to stay and get the civilians out. *This is gonna get ugly.*

Babe's mind toiled with the what-ifs regarding war, the current state of the economy, the government, and the increasing blatant crime. As he got in the truck, he called Trinity, "Still got your phone in ya back pocket while behind the bar. Naughty girl. Remember Daniel?" She did. "If he gets there before me, tell him I'm on my way. Is Samantha working tonight? I noticed she's been there several times with you and Finn." The answer was yes, she was there. "Maybe you could introduce her to Daniel. Let her know he's an amputee. Some people get freaked out."

"Why you wanna do your friend like that?" She sounded disgusted.

"Because I think he needs to get laid. Understand?" She answered she did, and Sam might fit the bill. He parked in the hotel to keep off the dark streets. Trouble was abounding, and it seemed he always had to watch his back and fend off ne'er-do-wells. Even as a kid, random students would try to pick fights. Only during his time as a Marine was there a level of peace other than that of the enemies they were fighting. Maybe because Marines focused on the task at hand, they didn't have time to worry about bucking up to the big guy; besides, they were all fucking appreciative he was on their side. Babe was a born leader, and often, because of a solid intestinal fortitude, those who were insecure felt the need to swipe at the leaders or talk trash, not so much as a Marine. His mind tumbled through his life as though keeping a score; he realized she was listening to him, waiting for some sign of conversation. "See you in a few, ma girl."

"Vic, you okay?" she worried. "You seem even more distracted than usual, and that's saying something, big man." There was a note of concern in her tone. Were the demons going to start up again? To her knowledge, it had been pretty peaceful, and the hallucinations had stayed at bay.

"Love you. Later." He said as he ended the call.

By the time Babe made it to Louie's, Daniel had not only arrived, but Samantha had latched onto him. Trinity looked at Babe, raised one shoulder, and blew him a kiss. It had been fifteen minutes tops since their phone conversation, and she'd managed to tee it up. Now, it was up to Daniel to strike it down the fairway. Daniel looked like a Marine, with a solid posture, broad-shouldered, muscular but thin, and with a short cropped high and tight. Babe figured he was probably popular with the girls in high school, although bordering on shyness. Losing his leg had not only done a number on his body but his self-esteem as well. It didn't have to be that way. He knew radically dismembered vets that had made themselves mentally whole. Yes, he lost his leg, but he made it home to live another day, and Uncle Sam took care of him with a career off the battlefield.

Babe suspected if he decided to re-enlist, the Marines would probably take him back gladly, but his window was closing as his birthday approached. He had a couple more years to make up his mind, but with how things looked, the Marines might come for him before. As it was, his superiors had called him a couple of times, and the psychologist always asked if he thought he was ready to return to service. *Say what? Are you nuts?* Nope, he was gonna be a dad and be home in case the fighting ever landed on his shores.

Trinity had his two-finger pour of Glenlivet waiting for him. Samantha batted her eyes, "You never told me you had such a handsome, available friend, Babe." *What to say? I thought you'd fucked every hard dick in the area; I guess you missed one.* Babe smiled; it was better than being rude. He saw the gleam in his wife's eyes and knew she had a good idea of what was roaming around in his mind. "And we've been making sure your little momma has been taking it slow." She batted her false eyelashes again with a snarky smile. *She better not push my girl too much, or she'll be getting bitch-slapped.*

"Congratulations, Captain. Trinity and Samantha told me all about the wedding and the baby. Excellent, sir. Thanks for meeting with me. I didn't know if you heard, sir. I had to see you because something horrible has happened." He cast his eyes downward, "Hurley ate his gun."

Babe pressed his head against the heel of his hand, closing his eyes. "What the fuck? He and I talked a month ago, maybe two, and he seemed okay. He had a great job protecting the elite when they went on a two-day gig. Ya know, rubbing elbows with the rich and famous. Man, he had it all—looks, smarts, charm, a cosmo kind of guy. He was one helluva Marine." He threw back the rest of his drink and tapped the bar. She cocked her head, looking deep into his eyes. His eyes glossed over with tears he wouldn't let fall. Trinity returned with his drink. He held the tumbler up, "Here's to you, Hurley. You served proud, semper fi." Collins held his glass up, saying semper fi. They both had a distinct faraway gaze. Their heads filled with memories as they felt the devastation hitting home—too many warriors were biting the dust. It left a lump in Babe's throat, and his chest felt tight.

Collins had two empty glasses in front of him. Did he need liquid courage to approach him? "Sorry, I had to be the one to tell you, Captain. That's why I wanted to get together. Wait, that came out wrong. I wanted to give the sad news to you in person and not over the phone. Besides, I always like tossing back a few with you. Maybe the four of us can grab dinner together one night." Samantha was all over him, and it was easy to deduce Collins was gonna get lucky. Maybe he might make an honest woman out of her, but that was unlikely.

"When's the service?" That would be one funeral he'd attend. The men had served together for most of his time in the Marines. He wished he knew Hurley was having such a hard go of it. Unless a person served under the conditions they did, they couldn't grasp the totality of it. Almost everyone came back a little fucked up, if not a lot. Warriors were eating their guns every damn day. *Where you at, God?*

LIGHT'S OUT

$\mathcal{E}$verywhere he looked, there was nothing but bad news. Hurley's suicide took him back a few pegs. The man had seemed together last they spoke. Was he too harsh on him about the babysitting for the stars debacle? He knew he could be harsh, even brash at times. Is that why Hurley wouldn't talk to him? Had he confided in Hurley about his own demons and how, more than once, he'd considered ending it all? Maybe Hurley left a note with all the answers. As questions flooded his mind, Babe realized that other than the hundreds of days serving together, he had no idea about any of his people's lives. It wasn't like that; it was combat, or did they know each other's stories, but he didn't because he was aloof and introspective.

Babe called Daniel, "Collins, it's Vic."

"Yes, sir. How can I help you, Captain?" Daniel always answered the phone in an all-business solemn voice, but upon finding it to be the Captain, it was like he got a pep in his step.

Babe fiddled with some loose papers he had floating around his truck. "Collins, you can call me Vicarelli, Vic, or Babe; I'm not your Captain anymore. I've been bothered greatly by Hurley's suicide. The questions I have for you, even though we were only on a couple of missions together," *Fuck, I sound pathetic.* "Did you feel I was approachable? I don't even recall Hurley's first name. Thank you for telling me face to face and sending me the funeral information. Are you attending?"

He could feel the pensiveness through the phone. *I'm a fucking bastard.* "Sir, we all looked up to you and knew we could count on you. We could talk to you about anything. You even helped me write a letter to my girl after I got the Dear John." His heart lightened, releasing a single tear to roll down his cheek. "Sir, the only way I know Hurley's first name is because all that kinda shit passes through me. Otherwise, I'd be at a loss, as well. His name was Jackson James Hurley; his family called him Jack. He had two ex-wives but no children. He had a sister and a brother. That's about all I know. Yes, I'm going; wanna ride together? I don't know how many others know, but I've tried to call a few. Thank Trinity for introducing me to Sam. She's a sweet girl; we've been having a good time. Suffice it to say I'm not bringing her home to meet the parents. I know this sounds real dick of me, but her sister is smokin' hot, and not, um—"

Babe chuffed and said he understood, but indeed, he'd gotten into a messy situation. They arranged a pickup time, getting them to the funeral home twenty minutes before the service. It was enough time to say hello, exchange niceties, and sit.

The next few days were uneventful. Since Babe's comment about Markey's strength, she'd started paying more attention to him, which was probably not a good thing. He tried to keep his distance and appear busy, which he was for the most part. She'd find him with some ridiculous bullshit question about the job. She knew he was married and not up for the cheating game, but still, she persisted. He finally had to tell her he thought she should ask Glenn any construction questions. Markey appeared put off, maybe even pissed but said she'd start asking the boss. If she was trying to slam him or make him feel inferior, it didn't work. He had fish frying in a few pans, so offending Markey was not at the top of the list, nor was a condescending remark.

Daniel had kept him apprised of changes in the funeral arrangements as he heard them. Hurley's family had it scheduled for Friday, with visitation from nine to eleven and service starting at eleven. Babe offered to pick Daniel up from the Algiers complex around ten. *Dress blues, indeed.*

"Ooh, boy, look at you in them dress blues. Smokin'. Come here, hot man, give us some sugar." She could see the sadness and anger in his eyes and tried to lighten the situation, but she only received a half-hearted smile. Her man was in pain, and she could see the weight he'd put on himself with guilt, which put a squeeze on her heart and tears in her eyes. Yes, he was sad, and yes, it was horrible, but he had nothing to feel guilty about. *Typical Babe*, she thought, *to take on the world's shit.* "Vic, sit next to me," and patted the bed. She turned his head toward her so they were face to face. "Do you miss being in the Corps?"

He had to think about the answer; it wasn't a simple yes or no. Babe had implied to Antoine that he'd stick around and be an active and present part of the marriage and soon-to-be family. Did he miss the Corps? To be candid, yes, there were some aspects, but knew it was time for a younger man to fill his shoes. He didn't want to be a pencil pusher or rise anymore in the ranks than he had; no, it was boots on the ground or no boots at all.

Babe's mind surfed the waves of mission memories, mostly buried away but now resurfacing since the news about Hurley. Did he decide to leave the Corps because he felt the Corps had left him and those who had dedicated themselves to their country? One thing was for sure what governed the country and the way of the world was shit.

Men ceased being men; they were all worried about feelings and opinions, *fuck that.* At times, he wondered who had the stones in a relationship, especially after getting as close as he did to the interactions of the Spring Breakers the year before when Jessica Lambert died. They staged it to look like a murder when all it was was sex games and rampant promiscuity. Not thinking he was a prude by any means, he liked a casual fuck as much as the next person, but the whole orgy, threesome games hadn't been his jam—to think those would be the up-and-coming leaders of the country. *Entitled and spoiled, all of them.*

It was one fucked up world, and here he was, bringing a child into the mire and filth. They would instill values in their little girl and barricade the hoards of malcontents that would probably try to manipulate her. He thought, *manipulate this,* as he could see himself jamming his heavy heel into the balls of some snot-nosed, cocky little bastard. Trinity watched as Babe disappeared into his mind's secret chamber. "Sometimes, Vic, I think you looked drugged. Wherever you go, you turn off the rest of the world. We all reflect, but you dissect every thought you have. Chill, my man, and get them dress blues squared away. What you been thinkin' about?" She twisted her long locks into an updo and clamped it with a claw, eying him the entire time.

He hmphed, "You asked if I missed the Corps. The thought took me to the state of the world and the people that one day would be running the circus, which brought images of the snarky, to use your expression, Spring Breakers, leading to thoughts of our baby girl and how some prick would try to manipulate her and then I had total delight in crushing his sack with my heel. Fucking asshole." He puffed out his chest like he'd conquered the world, and for a few minutes, he was content. The world, according to Babe.

The drive to pick up Collins allowed him to rehash memories of being with Hurley. The man always seemed upbeat; who would have thought he was capable of suicide? Babe's reflections flashed like a projector, showing each time he had put the barrel of a gun to his mouth. Those moments seemed to happen when he felt he'd let others down. Was he seeking approval, needing approval, or was he empathetic instead of sociopathic? The docs got it all wrong.

Collins was waiting outside of the gate for him. Dress blues, no doubt, made a pretty picture. Both men were somber, but Collins was the first to speak aside from their immediate greetings. "Cap-uuh, Vic, have you ever contemplated suicide? Like, has the pain ever been so bad you felt you couldn't breathe, and you wished it had been you that got blown up?"

Staring straight ahead, Babe replied many times, and the guilt beat him mercilessly. Even with a great wife, a baby on the way, and everything he'd believed to be impossible, he still had those moments, feeling the pain of losing another in his command, blaming himself. "We've seen enough killing for several lifetimes. Call me if you ever have those thoughts, no matter the time. Thoughts of Hurley still blow me away."

The family opted to bury him in their burial plot. Babe felt a vice-like grip on his heart. If given a choice, where would he like to be buried when the time came? Who was he kidding? Trinity would never give him a choice. He should have died in Afghanistan; there was no reason he lived through the nightmare. It would have made things so much easier. He pulled in and parked.

Walking into Lake Lawn, they were but two of a sea of Marines. *What a great send-off,* he thought. Hurley had impacted many lives. In some ways, he felt surreal as he approached the vastness of blue. Many of the uniforms stood at attention and saluted. He didn't deserve salutes anymore; he didn't like them before separating and, sure as shit, didn't feel comfortable at present. Stoically, he recognized the decorum.

Hurley's family stood by the closed coffin. Babe and Collins approached, offering condolences. Collins had gotten familiar with the family and quickly introduced the Captain. Babe remembered meeting them years before. They were complimentary as to the special attention he had given Hurley. He felt undeserved respect, and once again, his chest felt like straps had a stranglehold, making it difficult to breathe, or so he thought. He could see the whispers among the rank, chin pointing him to some of the younger boots. Many, one by one, introduced themselves. *Awkward.* The question Trinity asked him popped into his head. Did he miss the Corps? Maybe that's what all the tightness and uncomfortableness was all about. He did miss the Corps, the regimentation, the clearly defined lines, and the orders to be followed or commanded. Many Marines had wives and children; it was the norm, but he'd given his word in a fashion to Antoine.

There was something special about the preciseness of military funerals. Both ex-wives were present and standing with the family. If he were a betting man, he'd lay odds; Hurley didn't keep it in his pants, thus the divorces. They were beautiful women, one a blonde and the other a brunette, each with bodies made for Playboy. The brunette reminded him of Carmen, Javier's sister-in-law, and a gnawing of guilt crept up his spine thinking of the encounter in Cartagena. Trinity had been crystal; she didn't want to know, and he really didn't want to tell.

Out the side of his mouth, Collins whispered, "Vic, see Hurley's ex, the blonde, that's what Samantha's sister looks like, no lie."

With utmost muffled breath, Babe replied, "Yeah, I'd want to tap that, too."

Following the service, Collins made a beeline to the blonde, expressing his condolences. She flirtatiously smiled, and he pulled out his phone. *Well done, Daniel; Hurley would have gotten a kick out of sniping his ex at his funeral.*

Babe was ready to get the formalities over. He needed to get home, change, and go to work. While his mind roamed back and forth from Hurley to the task at hand, the thought of re-enlisting shone like a lighthouse, its beacon guiding yet warning. His mind turned round and round like a carousel at an amusement park. No matter how hard he tried, he couldn't stay focused.

Trinity was napping when he arrived at the apartment. Silently, he removed pieces of the dress blues, careful to neatly hang them. Once stripped down to his boxer briefs, the symphony of thoughts scaled down to a three-piece jazz ensemble. No longer was he haunted by voices barking to re-enlist or doubting his purpose. *I'm gonna be a dad*. Perhaps the uniform had a hypnotic effect.

The bed creaked as she rolled over, the sheets tugging at her top, exposing a peek of her rounded breast. "How'd it go, Vic?" she groggily spoke mid-stretch.

"It was strange like I was back in the Corps. The attendance was remarkable." He sat next to her on the bed. "And how are you feeling?" She dreamily said good and rolled her body against him. "Little momma, I gotta get to work, but I'll see you around five-thirty, then I'll be off to Chestnut." She made a wisecrack, saying it was a wonder they ever made a baby. "A man's gotta do what a man's gotta do. I'd like nothing more than to slide into the bed with you, but you know I can't. Never known you to be a prick teaser, Trinity. I love you, and we'll catch up later." He leaned over and kissed her before leaving with his four-legged buddy.

She whispered, but loud enough for him to hear, "I have plans for your prick later," she sighed and rolled over, snuggling his pillow.

On his way to work, moving along the sidewalk and dodging people coming the other way, he felt something slowly moving behind him. The hairs on his neck began to bristle. *What the fuck now? As* he turned to face a possible assailant, he found Trey slowly driving behind him. He put the passenger window down. "We had another murder; this time, the bastard mutilated the man, even worse than before. I was on the way to your job site; I think I remembered him as part of your crew back with the dumpster dude investigation. The guy's name is Mitchell Thomas; does the name sound familiar?"

Babe nodded, and a picture flashed before him. Markey had come onto the other welder or provoked an altercation. Someway somehow, she'd gotten him alone. There was no doubt in his mind that Markey was the perpetrator. There would be one surefire way he could find out, but was he willing to go out on that limb? It wasn't as though he had proof; what could he tell Trey?

As they pulled up to the site, Babe thanked him for the ride while Trey opened the back door to let Gunner out. Both men walked into the office; Babe clocked in, and Trey addressed Glenn. He knew the incident would jar Glenn, and he would take it hard. After half an hour, Glenn called the crew to him and introduced Trey, remarking some probably remembered the detective from the Stan situation. Glenn was holding it together by a thread; it wouldn't take much for him to lose it. The news moved the crew, and the atmosphere took on a palpable heaviness. Mitchell was one to keep the site lively either with his thumping music or fancy dance steps. In some ways, the welder reminded him of Nigel Hawkins from a couple of his missions. The Marine with the strange English accent kept things light with his crazy, 'Confucious say' comments.

No doubt, Mitchell was like Nigel, creating a flashback where Hurley's boot caught a tripwire. The English-born Marine assisted Babe in freeing the boot without blowing them all to kingdom come. Fade back to reality.

Trey interjected, "We have had a few murder victims recently, all men, but that's not saying they wouldn't go after a woman. Be watchful and careful. I'll try not to keep you too long."

Everyone got back to work, but there was a constant buzz throughout the construction site. Babe saw Trey approach Markey. He'd love to know how that went and what his take on the woman was. Nothing had pointed to her as the perpetrator; Babe had a gut feeling. Now that the victim was a co-worker, he increased his awareness of Markey's oddness. When Trey was talking, Babe glanced at her body language and micro-expressions. Either she was stone cold, and he knew the beast of emotionless killing well; after all, he was the poster child, or she wasn't the killer, and he was dead wrong. One thing for sure: the chick wasn't playing with a full deck; not saying he was, but she was a strange motherfucker.

Trey approached Babe. "Can I pick your brain for a minute?" He was waiting for the "Where were you last night?" question, but maybe not. Trey pointed toward the unmarked car, and they started walking toward it. "You know most of the people on the construction site?" Babe set his jaw and nodded, trying to figure out where the conversation was going. "What's your take on the heavyset white guy? Good people or ignorant questionable character?"

Babe knew he had changed his expression because the question came totally out of left field, taking him off guard. James was a slob, out of shape, and uneducated, but he was a happy-go-lucky kind of person. It blew his mind that Trey got squirrely over the man.

"From your face, I'm barking up the wrong tree." Trey guessed. "I'm not saying the killer is necessarily part of this crew, but the pain inflicted and the gruesome manner of the stab wounds indicated to me someone had anger issues with the guy. The other murders were brutal, but this was beyond, like, personal, ya know." Trey shifted, leaning against the car. "This would've turned your stomach, and I know you've seen some shit." Babe stood still with his hands on his hips, thumbs tucked under his tool belt. The internal debate began about whether he should ask about Markey.

He turned so he was mainly facing away from the construction site and on an angle to Trey. Babe asked, "What's your take on Markey, the strongly built woman?" One side of his mouth turned up as though the detective had said something amusing.

Trey tucked his chin and adjusted his position, "The lesbian?" Babe gave him the short version of his first encounter with Markey. "You're telling me –"

The big guy tipped his head. "She basically let me know she was interested in a tumble. She has hit on most of the men onsite. No one wants to do her, except maybe Mitchell. I think he'd have stuck his in any kind of hole. He was funny with some wild dance moves but made no bones about taking every opportunity. Maybe he gave it a go with her." Trey commented he and Max would be back on Monday, maybe even taking a few of the people to the station for questioning. "Go for it. Maybe someone knows something that they won't say on site."

Babe returned to his work. An hour into it, he felt someone coming from behind. Markey had a wild look in her eyes, half-crazed. "What'd the police want with you? Did you tell him about us?" *Us?* "I know you're married, but I can tell when a man wants me and Vicarelli; you cannot deny it. I've seen you checking me out, wondering what I would look like naked and willing."

He flipped his hammer in his hand, trying to stay calm. He wanted to ask the bitch what the fuck was wrong with her. There was no way he'd given any indication he was the least bit attracted to her. She repulsed him. The message had to be delivered right; she was a loose cannon.

"Ma'am, I am married and have no desire to step out on my wife. If I've misled you, it was unintentional." She growled at him, saying he'd be sorry for leading her on, and she knew how to cut him to the quick, snapping her fingers. She knew where his wife worked. He'd had it. He tried the polite and direct professional approach; now it was time to do it his way. "I've done my best to remain cordial and show you respect, but you've pushed the envelope. Stay the fuck away from me and bitch you don't want to threaten me; I've dealt with much bigger, stronger, and crazier opposition than you. Go near my wife, and I will kill you." Her response was as cold as his, claiming he better watch his back. He'd heard that one before, and it landed the last person to threaten him in the dumpster.

At the end of the day, Babe checked in with Glenn, warning him about the altercation with the crazy bitch. With as many complaints as he'd had, he needed to fire the woman. They chewed a bit on how the family was holding up since Chance's death. Glenn locked the office, and as he and Babe started walking away, Markey came behind them swinging a two-by-four toward Glenn, clipping his ear. Glenn went down. Babe turned as the board came flying his way. He ducked down and tackled her legs. The woman fell solidly to the ground; she flipped over and scrambled for another two-by-four. Babe contorted his body to maneuver away from the board-swinging bitch. Losing his footing and on the way down, the nearest thing to grab was a piece of rebar off the ground, and he hurled it at the woman like a javelin. It went through her neck and out the back of her cervical spine, instantly severing the spinal cord. Glenn called emergency assistance, saying they needed cops and paramedics.

Markey's eyes bulged as her now paralytic body collapsed on the ground. Her breath came out in gurgles. Babe predicted in his mind that she might have three more minutes tops. Police units screeched to the site as he tended to Glenn's ear. The graze of the board took the tip of his ear off. Had he not turned when she came from behind, she would have cracked his scull with the two-by-four. If the strike had happened anywhere other than outside the office, it would have been hand-to-hand combat until incapacitation or death. No one knew what skills she had, and the big guy pondered whether he could go to blows with a woman; a tackle was one thing. Instinct told him most definitely it was the them or us mentality instilled by the Corps. Glenn had the crew keep all iron and large metal scraps in a pile by the office trailer as a safety precaution; some of the pieces could be razor sharp. The rebar stuck out from the mound as though extending its service. *Sheer luck*, he thought, but Babe was more concerned about Glenn's ear than anything. Markey had brought this all on herself, granted she was mentally unstable.

"Be still," Babe said to Glenn as he took his own shirt off, balled it up, and held it against Glenn's ear. Watching his boss slip into shock made him pull him closer to shed his body heat. "Breathe, you're okay. Paramedics will be here momentarily." Given his time in combat, with constant unexpected assaults, Babe wasn't rattled by the attack and, in some ways, felt sorry for the woman. He knew their tête-à-tête had put a match to the gasoline.

Since using his shirt on Glenn's wound, all he had on his top half was a snug wife beater. His phone buzzed. "Vicarelli." He held the phone between his shoulder and ear. "Yes, I'm involved, Trey. Not a good time;

my hands are full." Minutes later, Max pulled up as the paramedics were working on Markey. Babe surmised she wasn't dead but holding on by a thread. It would be his luck for her to survive, and he'd still be at the top of her target list or facing jail time even though it was self-defense.

Max approached, "Holy shit, you'd make a good Chippendale. If I looked like you, I'd be bare-chested in the hot or blizzard cold. What choo got to do with all this, Babe?" The Marine looked over his shoulder and thumbed behind him. They couldn't remove the rebar, or she'd bleed out fast. Max' eyebrows raised when he saw the metal rod sticking out of the woman's neck. "Yowza, Babe, you done that? It reminds me of a movie I saw on TV; I think the guy's name was Achilles. It was way back during chariots and stuff. The actor was that famous pretty boy, Brad Pitt. He'd fly through the air in slow motion and kill his opponent with a dagger. Did you fly through the air, big man? Man, she's fucked up."

Glenn interrupted, "No, he threw the dang thing from the ground like a spear. She hit me with a two-by-four; she took the top of my ear off." By this time, the paramedics had bandaged him up, had an open line on him, and tried to put him on a gurney. "I can walk, guys." Babe winked at him and told him to take the ride. "Vic, lock the place up."

"You got it, chief." Max hung around getting the story from Babe. "You shoulda sent her my way. She's big and muscular like a man, but I can't be picky these days. I'd be man enough to handle her," he puffed out his chest. The response perked Max's ears when Babe said he thought she was the serial killer. "Fuck me, that'd be my luck. Glad you didn't introduce us. Hey, you want a ride, it'll have to be in the back. I got a lotta shit in the front seat. He figured a lift might be the best answer since all he had on his top was a ribbed undershirt.

Max talked the whole way to Louie's. Babe needed to tell Trinity what happened and that he was getting a shirt and heading to the hospital, although he suspected Bethany was already on the way.

When he walked into Louie's in his wife-beater, Samantha came unglued. Trinity checked her fast. "Babe, what the hell? It's too cold outside for a tank top. You think it's summer? Boy, you've lost your mind." He quickly kissed her, tapped the bar, and patted the stool beside him. The crowd was nothing Finn couldn't handle, and Babe needed a minute to tell Trinity the story of Markey, Glenn's ear, and that he was on the way to the hospital. "So, Glenn's gonna be okay, right?" She called Bethany, who was already on her way to the Emergency Room. He could hear the hysterics from the other side of the phone. While her outgoing personality had brought him a bit out of his shell, his control and calm had rubbed off on his lady. He inwardly smiled as Trinity consoled Bethany. A year before, they both would have been screaming hysterically; now, it was only Bethany shrieking. Dramatic and prone to hysteria were good descriptive words for the Noelle family. Her dad was the only one with stoicism; after all, men were not supposed to cry. *Whoever came up with that bullshit should be put in front of a firing squad.*

A CALL AWAY

*A*few weeks passed, and Thanksgiving was upon them. Glenn's ear was healing nicely, and the family had settled down from the incident. As anticipated, Markey died, but she had put up a hell of a fight and survived three days, miraculously after the encounter. Even with the information about the incident, Trey and Max again called Babe to the police station. He arrived promptly for their nine o'clock meeting. Trey led him into one of the interrogation rooms. *Are you kidding me?*

Trey seemed apologetic. "We know what happened, but her sister is claiming wrongful death and wants you arrested. Max explained in detail to the woman about the situation and how her sister had swung a two-by-four, taking off part of her supervisor's ear, and he could press charges against her estate, but he hadn't pursued that avenue." Trey continued telling Babe about educating the sister about previous encounters and warnings. He questioned if the sister was aware of her mental instability. "I told her about your service to the country." Trey audibly sighed. "I don't want you to be shocked like we were, but the sisters looked identical; only Melody has long hair. The sister is older than Markey, or Margaret, as she calls her."

Babe sat staring at the table, the gears churning away in his head. "You gonna arrest me? It was self-defense, and Glenn has security footage of her assault on us. Advise the sister she might want to rethink the situation. Is she suing French Quarter Renovation and Development?" *Probably looking for a payday.*

The discussion went further, and Trey did not answer the question about an arrest. Babe asked if they ever checked into the murders of the men, and since her death, it was odd how the killings had stopped. He reminded Trey he was a lawyer and informed him he had an accomplished attorney as Second Chair. Babe said it was unfortunate how things went down as they did, but she was out to kill one or both of them. The case was unquestionable self-defense, and neither he nor the company would pay her one red cent. A handsome payday was not in her future.

Trey patted the air down, settling the situation. Agraged about the waste of time, Babe felt impending anger clenching in his stomach, and his heart began to pound, yet his face was void of expression. Rarely did anyone spot his thoughts or emotions. *See me now, docs.* "We get it, and I think the sister may be just as unstable. We aren't stirring the pot; we are only keeping you informed. As far as arresting you, my friend, not in the foreseeable future." The meeting was over, and he could get back to work. Thoughts of the military were becoming more and more appealing; there wasn't the incessant bullshit of civilian life.

Stepping out onto the street, a woman who could easily be Markey, the deceased, approached him. She held her eyes wide with a crazed look; the sclera was visible around the iris. Pointing her finger at him with angered jabs in the air, she snarled, "You're the bastard that killed my sister. You better watch your step, mister. Me and my brother are coming for you, best believe." He continued walking, ignoring her rant. "I hope you heard me." He wanted to tell her to fuck off but held his tongue and continued walking. The hurried pounding of her feet along the sidewalk sounded the alarm that he was about to be accosted. Babe swiftly turned, eyes glowering with dare, saying don't push me.

Trey exited the station house and saw the near confrontation. "Stop where you are," he said, holding his badge in the air. "NOPD, do not move." He approached the woman who was four feet from Babe. "Are you okay, Vic?" Babe lifted his chin, affirmative. "Ma'am, you cannot threaten people. I understand you are distraught, but your actions are out of line, and I could well arrest you for attempted battery, premeditated at that."

"Free to go?" Babe asked. Trey waved him on. The big guy hailed a passing cab and was gone in seconds. The whole thing was a cluster. He called Daniel. "Collins," Daniel responded before he could identify himself. He said he'd know the Captain's voice anywhere and what could he do for him. "I think I might want to re-enlist." For several minutes, Daniel went on about the procedure, which Babe already knew but listened to anyway. Then Daniel ended his encyclopedic instructions by asking if he was sure with a new baby on the way. *My fuse is getting too short, like a civilian, dammit,* he thought. "I'll get back to you."

Once at Conti, Babe called Trinity and told her to stay close to home and about the encounter with Markey's looney sister. Glenn overheard the conversation, waited for him to disconnect, and then grilled him on the sister and confrontation. Still, the hot topic on the construction site revolved around the near-death experience Glenn and Babe had with demented Markey. People stayed away from her because of her constant inappropriate offers and consequent threats after being declined—*drama, drama, drama.*

Other than an appointment with Trey and the confrontation with Crazy Sister, it must have been a familial trait; he headed for his truck and Chestnut. There was no point in going to Louie's; he had asked her to stay home.

He had a quickening of dread the whole drive home, and following his gut, he turned the truck around for Louie's. Finn was scrambling at the bar. *Early for this kind of crowd,* he thought. He told Babe, "She's been in there for a long time," and thumbed toward the restroom.

Babe rapped on the door, cracked it open, and called in; there was no answer. He barged through the door, finding Trinity crumpled on the floor with blood pooled under her head. "Trinity," he shook her, then felt for a pulse. It was weak and thready. He called nine-one-one and then yelled to Finn. "Shut the bar down; no one leaves, tell Shep." Finn ran into the ladies' restroom and saw Babe crouched next to her lifeless-looking body with a pool of blood underneath her head. "Was there a big blonde girl here?" He said she was sitting with some big dude at a corner table. Paramedics and police arrived within minutes; he told them to go to Touro if they thought she could tolerate the ride. Babe called Antoine as he made his way to the table of the blonde woman and man. "You picked the wrong fight and the wrong woman," he growled.

Babe threw the man against the wall, his forearm against his neck. The police tried to separate the men. It took two of them. He whispered in the ear of the blond-haired man, spewing as though the devil himself, that he was a dead man. The woman started to walk out when Max entered. "No, ma'am, sit your ass down now." Babe saw Big Paul and Antoine Sr. entering the bar. Babe looked at her dad, tipped his chin, acknowledging him, then pushed past everyone and jumped in the ambulance with Trinity. Hands tried to grab him, but he managed to avert them all. Max knew he'd come in peacefully when he was damned good and ready. While that was not by the book, the detective highly regarded and respected the Marine. He also knew Babe could have created far more havoc than thrusting someone against the wall.

Sirens blared as the ambulance gassed it to the University Medical Center; the paramedics took her to the closest place for immediate attention. He knew what that meant; she was in dire straights. *Here's Your big chance, God. From what I read in your Good Book, You do not negotiate, but don't let my lady die, and I'll do whatever you want me to—take me instead.* Babe touched her leg as the medics worked on her. "Trinity, I'm here."

"Kell, she's crashing." The young, tall drink of water gripped the fluid bag and squeezed it. His knuckles blanched as he applied pressure to the solution. "C'mon, Missy, we're almost there." The medics looked at each other; Babe could read the situation was crucial, and there was a good chance he was gonna lose her.

He wiggled her foot. "Ma girl, fight, c'mon Trinity, you gotta do this." The ambulance pulled in, and with massive expediency, they had her out of the vehicle, shouting stats and information to the awaiting team, who whisked her off, he speculated, to surgery. Everything was moving fast. It all seemed like a horrific nightmare. Babe easily kept up with them, not taking his eyes off Trinity. She looked lifeless. He understood some of the information imparted, and he knew enough to scare the shit out of him. It looked bad, really bad.

"Sir, you gotta wait here. We'll update you as soon as we can." He could've burst through the door but respected command and would wait for news.

The situation was complete pandemonium, and no one would give him any answers. It was as though he was invisible. Nobody consulted with him or took time to tell him what was going on or where they were taking her.

Babe grabbed one of the nurses. "That's my wife. What's going on; stop for a second and talk to me. Where are they taking her? Tell the docs she's pregnant." He thought her condition was apparent, but he'd seen other women with pot bellies that one could easily misconstrue as pregnant. The nurse responded there was no time to waste and that she'd get back to him as soon as they had answers. *No time to waste? Fuck no!*

Another hospital employee tapped him on the arm and asked him to follow. The man was kind, asked him if he needed anything, and led him to a private cubicle. Babe answered question after question; no, he didn't have her insurance card. Yes, she had insurance. When asked for name and address, as Babe answered, there was a slight indication of name recognition from the registration guy. Did she have a Living Will? Even though the man was pleasant, Babe was impatient and wanted answers to his questions. His phone rang, and it was Antoine. "I have to take this; it's her father," Babe answered the call, spoke fast, and apprised him of the situation. He could hear the concern in the man's voice when he told him they were at University. Giving reassurance, her father said their family of prayer warriors and Father O'Shea would arrive soon. "Yes, sir." He told Babe to pray, and he had Big Paul taking care of business; the Marine needed to be with Trinity and not worry about the scum. It would be a done deal.

Antoine and Big Paul went into the kitchen with Shep. "Nathan, you know what happened?" He looked intently, hands folded in front of him with Big Paul beside him.

"No one knew anything until Babe came looking for Trinity. Finn said she'd been in the ladies' room, and the Marine went in and found her. Someone accosted her in the bathroom, Antoine. I dunno if it was the big blonde woman or the man, but as you seen, your son-in-law had the man against the wall. All's I can say is they fucked with the wrong girl. She's tough, Antoine; she'll be fine. I know you're gun-shy since Chance. Who could blame you?"

Antoine Sr. paced back and forth, searching for the appropriate answer. He knew Trinity's man would not sleep until he had exacted suitable punishmment, which, in all likelihood, would spell death.

"Tell the cops I want the man and woman in the office back here. I'll be waiting." Shep went into the bar, told Max, and just like that, the police escorted the woman and man to the back. The two seemed antsy and apprehensive. With a hardened appearance, Antoine asked, "You know who I am? You don't want to fuck with my family or me. Everyone knows about the Noelle family. I don't know which of you hurt my girl, but because you were both in on the planning, you'll pay the price one way or another." He looked over his shoulder at Big Paul, "Take 'em out the back door and hold 'em at the safe house. If my girl doesn't recover—" he closed his eyes and slowly opened them.

The woman stammered, "That goon killed my sister. He's a monster."

"Your sister had it coming. You better hope my baby recovers." He waved his hand toward the door, "Big Paul, take a few guys with you. Give Inez my best. Do what needs to be done."

Babe's senses felt like he was on a merry-go-round. There had been a copious amount of blood. Who knows how long she'd been unconscious? Would her brain have been oxygen-deprived for too long? What about the baby? He knew her breaths were shallow, barely any movement to her seemingly lifeless body. Antoine had to be beside himself. Thoughts bounced around like the ball in an NBA game. He knew severe head trauma could manifest in many ways. Any or all of the senses could be impaired. Staring at the floor, he began a silent pleading prayer. *I know we haven't been that close, but you have helped me many times, and while I never understood why bad things happen to good people, one could speculate I never wondered why good things happened to bad people. Is it just shit happens, and you're there one way or the other, picking up the pieces? Trinity's hurt and needs your help. I'm not asking for me or even our baby, but for her. Please help her. Save her. I know You are good and the only one who can save her. I pray for her family; they've been through a ton of shit. Please bring her back to her family.*

He heard the sound of feet approaching. The whole Noelle clan, minus Antoine Sr., had arrived. Mama Noelle went straight to him and wrapped her arms around his head. Something happened that had never happened before; he couldn't hold back the tears. "Suga, all we can do is pray. You can lean on us; we're your family and are here for you." Here was this woman with her child on death's doorstep, mothering him. It felt strange but warm, undefinable inside. Was it a mother's love that felt gentle beyond words and comforting? She petted his hair and back with loving strokes. He gathered himself, stood, and offered her his chair. She accepted and sat. He began pacing as he knuckled the tears from his eyes. *What was that outpouring of feeling?*

Babe crouched next to her. "Thank you, ma'am." If this was what people called warm and fuzzy, then maybe it came close; the feeling was definitely unusual.

"I know you're tough, but a mama can see the soft goodness inside, like a fine chocolate. Our girl has lost a lot of blood—"

"She can have all they need from me." She smiled at him. The big, calloused Marine loved her girl.

She tipped his head toward hers, "Dawlin, it can't be just any blood. Trinity is A-positive, which is common. We'll find what she needs." She stroked his cheek and got up. "We'll see you tomorrow, I suspect," she said as she started to walk away.

"Ma'am, I understand blood typing and match. I'm what they call a universal donor; I'm O-negative. As I said, she can have as much as they'll take." He stood in front of her, looking down. "Y'all are so good to me; Trinity is my everything, and I'll do whatever is required. I'll see you in the morning." He walked her to the elevator, where her driver waited for her. Antoine Sr. had not made his appearance in the waiting area yet. Was he dealing with Inez or some business call, or most likely, he was attempting to keep it together and needed some quiet time? He found it curious that her mother left. Was it too much for her to handle, or was there another pressing issue he should be taking care of, and she took charge? Time would tell.

After returning to his seat, Babe called Mays, who answered immediately. "Hey, little brother. Everything okay in New Orleans?" Babe poured out the story and again started to choke on his words. He began with all the what-if questions. "Wait to worry, Babe, or you'll be worrying twice over the same thing. Wait for the doctor's advice before weaving the narrative without the facts. Man, y'all live in a fucking soap opera; not criticizing, just observing. It's a different version of the drama over here. Are you praying?" Babe affirmed he was. "Good. Keep on praying. I know you have a hard time, but you can fake it til you make it, and brother, God hears those prayers, too." He'd heard that advice from his wife recently. They agreed to check in the following day.

The hours ticked over slowly without a word from the doctors or nurses. He felt sure they had to know something. Three mismatched chairs were against the back wall as though there was nowhere else to place them. Babe sat in one. Bethany moved next to him and held his hand. "You saved my Glenn, and for that, I shall always be grateful. We will be by your side. My sister is a fighter; she will pull through this. It might take time, but she'll make it. You need to believe." He gave her a half-cocked smile. Something had changed in him—emotional in her mother's arms, choked speaking with his newfound brother, feeling lost and vulnerable. Where had the silent, controlled, and in-charge Marine gone? It was as though the incident stripped his armor away, leaving him naked and frightened.

Trinity's brothers sat in a row facing the first section of seating. They saw the doctors first. At the same time, Antoine Sr. walked into the waiting room. The man approached the surgeon while everyone else sat. *Oh, hell no.* Babe got up and stood by Antoine. The doctor said the next twenty-four hours were crucial, but she was a strong young woman. Babe felt it would be insensitive to ask about the baby, but Antoine voiced concern. The doctor's response could not have been any better. Surprisingly, the baby was perfect and unaffected. He asked who Babe was, and Antoine quickly said Trinity's husband.

Babe detected skepticism in the doctor's micro-expressions. "Sir, quite often with this kind of trauma, there can be—"

The big man stood still except for his hands, which clenched and released nonstop. A thought would zing, and he'd ball into a fist, then as quick as it came, it went, and his hand would release. Antoine watched, wondering if this was some protective mechanism or if the man wanted to hurt someone, and if so, he certainly understood. Inez and Big Paul would see to the details; the Marine had enough on his plate. "No disrespect, but I'm aware of the possible ramifications of brain trauma. I've seen it too many times, sir. I also understand the twenty-four-hour window is relevant to physical health and not the mental aspect. I've seen it range from amnesia to full-on personality changes. I realize there is a broad spectrum of possibilities." The surgeon nodded. Babe's size and build gave some people the thought of having all brawn and no brain, but such was not the case, and the doctor realized it quickly. Babe was a sharp knife, not a dull blade. The waiting game continued. It was all in God's time if the entity held the strings like a puppeteer. Trinity would ream his ass if she heard him compare God to some sideshow. *Sorry, God. Sometimes, most times, I don't get it.*

Most of the family waited a few hours and trickled out to their homes and families or significant others one by one. Although not vocalized, it was apparent they all felt the loss of Chance, their brother, and the situation brought up those raw, painful memories. It was like a perpetual silent vibration running through the family members with unspoken words. Babe sat, arms folded against his body and feet flat on the floor. He stayed in the same position for hours. A nurse approached, telling him she'd call if there were any changes. He thanked her but continued to sit. One thing the Marines taught well was the ability and patience to wait. He could sit perfectly still for hours without a twitch of a muscle.

Although slight, he could hear the almost undetectable tick of the clock's hands as they moved and the flip of someone's digital timepiece. The what-ifs started to scream. He slammed his hands on his thighs as though refusing to let the mind game win. He pulled up the Bible app on his phone. He remembered the night he installed it on his phone, waiting outside the Holiday Inn Beach Resort in Pensacola waiting for Chop, his comrade and helo pilot. What a pathetic excuse for a man he turned out to be. Babe wished he had never seen the drug dealing, human trafficking nefarious side of the pilot. The life-saving heroic memories faded when he saw the true nature of the man. He shook off the thought.

As time passed, Trinity's mother returned to the waiting room, sitting by Antoine Sr. The two whispered back and forth; he guessed the woman couldn't sleep or had to settle something at the house. Hours went by without word or change. Mama Noelle sat, moving her fingers from one bead to the next of her Rosary. Babe stayed seated, occasionally glancing at Antoine. They were the only three people in the waiting room. News came that Trinity was out of recovery, still unconscious but breathing on her own. The staff transported her to the ICU. Unlike before with Chance, the nurses let them all into the ICU. She looked like Sleeping Beauty—peaceful perfection. The doctors couldn't say or predict when she would wake or if she would regain consciousness. Mama Noelle leaned forward and kissed her forehead. "You sleep, my baby. We'll be back in the morning." She signaled for Babe to come closer to her as she whispered for him to go home and rest. He agreed but had no intention of leaving the hospital. Not having a chair in the room clearly indicated that the hospital meant for visits to be brief. He walked the Noelle's to the elevator and said he'd see them in the morning. Once again, Mama Noelle encouraged him to go home.

"Sir," he addressed Trinity's dad. "Would you let me know if you hear from Inez or Big Paul? I have a vested interest in this matter, as you well know." Antoine confirmed as he stepped onto the elevator. Babe returned to the ICU waiting area. The nurse brought him a cup of coffee, offering a pillow and blanket. "I'm good, thank you."

Babe sat staring into space, which roused the demons to pry into the void of his mind. *Did you really think you'd have a happily ever after?* They echoed Javier's comment. *The authorities were correct; it was a serial killer, just not the one they thought. Everyone around you dies; you're like the Grim Reaper.* He leaned the back of his head flush with the wall, rocking his skull against the wall. He opened the Bible app and began reading. God was the only one who could rid the demons; that's what Trinity told him. This would've never happened if he hadn't entered Trinity's life, but maybe she would've never been rescued from her ex's brother. *Read. Read. Read.* It would be the only source of peace for the moment.

"Inez, has Big Paul shown up yet?"

"Oh, Antoine, I'm so sorry, she'll be okay, dawlin'. Your girl is hard-headed like you. We praying for her. Yes, Big Paul is here, and those two are taking a dirt nap. You tell your Marine son-in-law he don't need to worry 'bout a thing. We made sure they suffered plenty. When we finished with them, they's momma couldn't have recognized them. Get you some sleep. Y'all got a road ahead with Trinity, from what I hear."

"Thank you for everything. I'll pass the word along to Babe."

A WAITING GAME

Days turned into two weeks, and she showed no sign of waking. He'd touched base with Ruthie. He only left to grab a quick shower and an on-the-run bite. Hours upon hours, he'd sit in the same chair, occupying his mind with reading, FB trash, and texting his frenemy, Javier. Still engrossed in his Bible app, he heard distant footsteps and figured it was someone from the ICU. They would get him every hour for a ten-minute visit. It wasn't like she was awake or moving, but he could have looked at her forever, trying to will her awake. The steps became louder, and when he looked up, it was Mays. "Hey, little brother." The two clutched tightly to each other. "How are you, and how is she?"

Skipping the subject, Babe commented, "Damn, you look good. How much have you lost?" Babe chucked him on the arm. Gripping his bicep, he remarked, "You exchanged it all for muscle. You must be hitting the weights like a madman."

Mays laughed at his comments, sat beside him, and started with the questions. Babe gave him the story, which he'd already done in the initial phone call, but it meant more in person, and he felt much better. The brothers spoke for hours, filling in all the details of their lives since Babe left Atlanta. Mays waited patiently each time Babe went in to see Trinity. He hoped he'd find her with eyes open and a sassy smile each time he entered her hospital room, but Trinity lay still with the look of death. He stayed the allotted ten minutes, petting her hand and whispering words of love. There were no two ways about it; love was a powerful thing.

The nurse touched his shoulder. It wasn't until then that he realized the ten-minute visit was more for the family than the patient. Only God knew when she'd wake up. For family and loved ones, it was a crap shoot as to whether she would be a form of herself or an entirely different version. It was a wait-and-see proposition, which normally wouldn't have made him break a sweat, but the unknown in this instance was terrifying.

Mays stood, meeting him halfway. "You look like shit. The nurse and probably everyone else has your number; you gotta get out of here. It's dang near six. Is this what you do every day? C'mon; they'll call you." He grabbed Babe's shoulder. "I'm starving, and you look like you could use a meal and a punching bag. I'd venture to say you haven't been working out or sleeping at home in bed." Babe walked with him to the elevator, not saying a word. The lump in his throat felt permanent, as did the weight of a punishing boot on his chest. Could everyone around see how labored his breaths were? Try as he might, the deal with Markey was not his doing. He wasn't going to sucker into a self-loathing blame game. It was easier to hate himself than blame someone else. He had shouldered beratement and could push back; he had to find the Marine in himself. The feelings factor was relentless; he remembered how easily he could say, fuck feelings; they're overrated. The intensity of love was euphoric, but the other side of the coin, loss, ripped his guts apart, tearing at his heart and vanishing his will to survive.

Mays broke the silence, "Bro, I took a cab from the airport, so you'll have to chauffeur me." He smiled with the same crooked smile that Babe had. Babe led the way to his vehicle. "Why not?" pointing to the truck. "Of course, you have the most badass motherfucking truck on the road." He chuffed.

A phrase he learned from Trinity, Babe said, "Let's not get hysterical." He waited a moment in thought, then spoke, "Far helped pick the truck out. The old guy was a trip and a half. It's been some time since you've been to the old homestead—it pretty much looks the same, except I have three boys stirring havoc." The brothers reminisced about their grandfather. It was shocking how much Mays remembered, stating Babe resembled the old guy. It was uncanny, other than the coloring, which was from their father.

He pulled into the driveway. "Shit, Bro, it looks the same, except the absolute curtain of silence and stillness has evaporated, and life emanates from the place. You said the caretaker's name is Ruthie?" he nodded.

A sumptuous aroma filtered from the house. As soon as they walked in, a cheerful voice called from the kitchen. "Chicken stew tonight; I hope that's to your liking." She rounded the corner and was startled upon seeing Mays. "Lord, have mercy if you don't look like pictures of your momma, boy. Your brother has told me all about you. I'll set another place." She chattered on about the boys. She called up to them. After mentioning that Babe was home, they came down like a herd of buffalo, stopping short when they saw Mays.

Before any of the boys started with the weird looks and sizing up Mays, he introduced them. Always off the cuff, Reg said, "No fuckin' way, there's two of you? What the—" Ruthie's throat clearing brought hushed giggles from the boys.

"You betta have ya money for the jar. You almos' had two infringements," Chris pointed out. They were full of questions. "Dude," he said to Babe, "He's dang near as big as you; I mean, he's as tall but not obscenely muscled like you."

Babe put his hand up to stop the remarks and asked Chris what was up with the new vocabulary—infringements and obscenely. The other two laughed, saying, "Merritt Lancaster." Studly Chris had evidently moved on and had a new girlfriend. Jacob polished the comment by saying the new girl was a brainiac with big jugs. Their giant hero cocked his head to the side with a look that screamed, "Really?" After washing up, everyone took a seat at the table. The boys hit Mays with question after question. Babe had a hard time paying attention; he didn't like being away from the hospital. The what-ifs consumed his thoughts. The questions hit all corners. *What if she wakes up and I'm not there? What if she spikes some complication, and I'm not there? What if she was scared and alone?*

Ruthie watched him like a protective mother, fearing he'd head down a rabbit hole. Her fear was that he would one day go down the hole and not return. This tragedy with Trinity might be the straw that breaks his back. She instructed the boys to take plates to the kitchen, asked for Mays, and then took Babe's. "You hardly touched your plate. How you gonna be big and strong for when your wife gets better? It won't be long after that til the baby comes. You need to keep up your strength. Go on and take ya shower." Babe didn't argue or even reply. "So, you from Atlanta?" She smiled at Mays with warmth. "I've never been there. I hear it's nice once you away from the city, but isn't that the way everywhere?" She heard Babe's door close. "Honey, I'm worried sick over your brother. I have never seen him like this, and I understand what war and tragedy can do to a person. My son, Clive, was in the military, and it took him time to get well, but this with Miss Trinity is something else. He is not himself, I tell ya. Maybe you being here might help." She cast her eyes downward, shaking her head. "Dear God, I pray for him every night. I hope she wakes up soon."

Mays said he understood and had no doubt that his brother would come out on the other side. The way he understood the story, it was a mess from the beginning on the job site. They spoke until Babe came down.

"You can stay here. Ruthie will show you your room. If you need clothes, you can borrow mine. I didn't see a suitcase." Mays rolled his eyes and said he forgot to get it from baggage claim; all he could think about was getting to Babe. "How about you drop me off at the hospital and get your luggage from the airport? Then come back here, and I'll see you in the morning if you feel like coming to the hospital."

Ruthie suggested they both ride to get the luggage as the new airport was complicated or so she heard. Then, Mays could drop him off at the hospital or keep him company in the waiting room. "I brought my backgammon set; we can play rather than count the tiles on the floor or ceiling. I'll take a quick shower, and you decide."

The trip to the airport was quiet. Mays brought up his ex-wife and how he'd not heard from her. He couldn't understand how she could abandon them so easily. He told Babe he had to start talking and not locking himself in his head. The one-sided conversation moved to working out and how it would be inspiring to see Babe work out. "Okay, dude, we will just ride in silence. Whatever you got going in your head needs to stop. I came here to support you, but I'm useless if you don't talk." Babe looked over at him and then back at the road. Soon, they pulled up to the baggage claim area. "I got an idea; you sit here and think up some things to say while I get my bag."

With a half-cocked smile, Babe turned and said, "Fuck you."

"Thank God, the mute speaks." Mays jogged to the entrance.

Babe called Javier and briefly spoke. Random questions popped into his head, he guessed from some inner insecurity. The shrinks would have a field day with him. *Captain Vicarelli, have you always had this feeling of incompetence? Did you feel like your mother loved you? So, you say you feel like you are on an island alone and naked? Have you always felt this way?* "Hey, Marine, if you want to do some heavy breathing, you picked the wrong person; it doesn't get my dick hard. You either talk to me or get the fuck off the phone. You better get your shit together. Friend, you are on quite a few hit lists, including mine," he lightly chuckled. "Seriously, it's a dangerous position to put yourself in such a consumed position. Think about these words of advice. Your girl—"

Babe interjected, "Pregnant wife."

Javier snapped back with viper-like speed and searing pain, "Creating an even greater urgency. You are vulnerable on too many levels. As easy to get as a civilian." Mays returned to the truck with his case and garment bag, shrugging his shoulders as if to ask who was on the phone.

"Gotta jet." He ended the call and responded to Mays. "Javier."

"You call some cartel thug and open up when I flew to be at your disposal. Isn't he the guy who wanted to kill you?"

Babe pulled from the curb just as one of the airport security guards approached them. "Still does. He wants to, but for some reason, can't or is biding his time, like a cat toying with a mouse. Hell, he flew me home on his private jet." His phone lit up, and he put his finger in the air, "It's Antoine." He answered, "Yes, sir?"

"Marine, she opened her eyes briefly, but it's a good sign. I thought you might like the update. The nurse said it could be involuntary, but I bet she's trying to wake up." Babe thanked him and said he was fifteen minutes away. He punched the accelerator, weaving through the traffic. Mays constantly stomped on an imaginary brake and braced himself for what he imagined was the makings of an accident.

"You want me to get out when we get there, and you take the truck home to Chestnut?" Babe asked.

From the passenger seat, it was easy for Mays to reach back to his bag. When he faced forward, he had a backgammon case. "Told you and watch the road; you drive like a maniac."

The neurologist called Mama and Papa Noelle into a private room. They sat on a sofa as he pulled up a chair. "I'm not going to sugar-coat the situation. Mr. and Mrs. Noelle, we are seeing some amazing brain activity and responses to stimuli. This is encouraging, but no one knows the outcome." They wanted to know what to expect; what would be the next good sign to look for? The doctor had documents in one hand and the other resting on his knee. His bedside manner wasn't overly comforting, but he wasn't cut and dry with no emotion or facial expressions. Whether his kindly appearance was a charade for such discussions or it was his nature, Antoine couldn't read. He took a pen out of his pocket to review the test results.

Babe exited the truck and told Mays he'd see him inside or know he was on the way to Chestnut. An elevator was open for once without a queue trying to get on board. He cautiously speculated Trinity's progress as the elevator passed each floor with a ding. He hauled ass to the waiting area for the ICU. One of the nurses came from behind the station and led him to the private room. She knocked, and the door opened. He saw her parents on the sofa. He was hesitant to think they seemed better than before. Maybe the doctor had good news. "Sir, can you read me in?"

Antoine lowered his head in a slow nod of agreement. The neurologist sketched the basic information he'd imparted to her parents. Then he held one of the test compilations, pointing to different colored pathways on a graph, describing what each meant, but carefully stating it was all a matter of time. Given her condition upon arrival at the hospital, the news was better than anyone would have expected. All in all, the report implied good news but also the harrowing possibilities. Mama Noelle was quick to acknowledge the situation was in God's hands. The doctor neither confirmed nor denied her comment. Babe could understand the man's thinking. The meeting concluded, and the three returned to the waiting area.

Mays had the backgammon set up and smiled as Babe came his way. Before sitting, he introduced his brother to Trinity's parents. Antoine replied with wrinkles creased along his forehead, "I didn't think you had family." He was checking Mays out with a discerning eye.

Babe put his hand on Mays' shoulder for a light squeeze. Looking directly into Antoine's eyes, he explained, "It's a long story, but the gist is we recently discovered each other. We share the same biological parents. I told you my father was an abusive alcoholic, and for now, we can leave it there unless you want all the gory details. It's been a blessing for both of us." Babe figured if he used the churchy terminology to ring the bell,

Antoine might pass on by with a nice to meet you and a handshake. As hoped, it was the exact response. Mays and Babe approached Trinity's mom for introductions. Once all settled, the brothers sat for a game of backgammon to while away the hours.

STRUCK SIDEWAYS

*B*abe had to admit having Mays around did lighten the load. Like the perfect key to a rusty lock, Mays opened Babe's heart, filled with fear, unsettled issues, and an undying first and only love.

Heads against the wall, the brothers propped their legs on chairs in front of them; both men had fallen asleep. Trinity's nurse softly shook Babe, who then elbowed Mays. "Your wife is awake. Her mother is with her and has another five minutes. You'll be able to go in after. Babe was on high alert, his heart pounding with anticipation. He stood and began to pace. Mama Noelle came out, trails of dried tears along her cheeks. He was ready and didn't want to wait to speak with Trinity's mom, but approached her.

She seemed shaky. "Sit with me a minute, hon." The tears began to flow again. "She's not right. She keeps asking for Chance and Joey. When I tried to explain that both had died, she refused to believe my words. When I mentioned she was married to you, she went hysterical, saying no and crying. Honey, she has no idea who you are. She is confused. Maybe seeing you might remind her; I wanted you to be aware of what you're walking into." Her voice hitched. "I'm so sorry. She hasn't acknowledged she's pregnant yet. Guard your heart, honey."

"Yes, ma'am." He closed his eyes, accepting the possibility that seeing him wouldn't jog a memory. "Thank you." He walked with dreaded steps toward the ICU. The staff cast their eyes downward as he proceeded to her room. He swallowed hard, took a deep breath, and slid the door open.

He smiled at her. "I'm happy to see you've woken up. You must feel very confused, and that's par for the course—"

She cocked her head, interrupting him, "Who are you?" Trinity stared at him; her eyes rolled back in her head, and she was gone. Monitors beeped out of control; people rushed helter-skelter; this was his worst nightmare.

All he could think was, *Wait, no, no, no. Someone do something. Save her. Where are you, God?*

The Big What-Ifs

Will Trinity regain her memory and remember Babe?
What did Antoine mean by getting on with his life? Does he know some secret?
Will Babe give up hope and re-enlist?
How will Trinity deal with being pregnant?
Will Babe ever be able to see his daughter?
Will Mays and Babe go to Norway?

Last tidbit for thought…

Will flags be raised about Markey's missing sister and brother, forcing Babe's hand to seek refuge and find a new life in Cartagena?

All these postulations will be answered in the fifth book of the **FIT THE CRIME** series, *The Impostor Lie*.

Visit my website, corinnearrowood.com. Reviews are appreciated, and I love hearing from you. I hope you are enjoying the metamorphosis of this character.

As always, I wish you love! Corinne

Many Thanks

To my husband, Doug, the love of my life for over thirty-seven years, thank you for patiently waiting while I finish one more thought, which turns into a chapter hours later. Your support and encouragement give me the boost to continue my passion. Three more books to go to finish the series, not a promise, just a maybe.

Thank you to our children and their husbands and wives, for cheering me on, attending my release events, and inviting your friends. The more, the merrier makes for a great party.

Thank you to our fabulous grandchildren who tell everyone their Nana is an author. (I hope the three littles will follow in their older cousins' footsteps)

I don't think I've mentioned the Lunch Bunch. Bobbie, Kaki, Betsy, Susie, Kit, and the occasional surprise of Mary Catherine, y'all have been onboard with me since the first story. Great lunches, lots of laughs, and heartfelt conversation—Thank you, ladies, for your friendship and willingness to hear my incessant chatter about new storylines. I love our Wednesday lunches, and one day, I will write *Tales of Time and Wisdom* delivered by the Lunch Bunch.

Thank you, Paige Brannon Gunter, for being the editor I need. You've taught me more than you know. I can always count on your honest opinions and suggestions. You help me keep continuity in my books, catch the uh-ohs, and respond when I need a jump start. I love that you love the characters and appreciate their growth. Hopefully, you will be my forever editor.

Thank you, K.N. Faulk, for continuing to edit my work with love. I look forward to more adventures together.

Words cannot express my appreciation to Cyrus Wraith Walker. He understands what I want as a cover design even when I can't describe it. You are absolutely amazing and bubbling over with talent. You are the real deal! Thank you for creating each book as a work of art.

To the readers who have followed my journey, I cannot express my appreciation enough, and I hope I continue to quench your desire for adventure and relationships with my characters. I hope you enjoyed *The Inevitable Lie* and look forward to Book Five, *The Impostor Lie*.

I cannot express my utmost gratitude to the men and women of the Armed Forces for their dedication, courage, and resolve to protect our country. It is with heartfelt thanks to the families and friends of our brave men and women of the Armed Forces, who sacrifice so much. Our prayers are with you and your loved ones.

The statistics of PTSD are staggering. Many of our Marines and soldiers come home entrenched in the horrors they experienced and the nightmares they cannot escape. If you know one of our heroes who might be suffering from PTSD, contact the Wounded Warrior Project, National Center for PTSD, VA Caregiver Support Line at 888-823-7458.

Statistics show there are between 13 and 15 veteran suicides every day. Pray for our men and women of the Armed Forces and support them as they return home. Get help from the Veterans Crisis Line. Call 988 (Press 1) or text 838255.

Other Books by the Author
Censored Time Trilogy
A Quarter Past Love (Book I)
Half Past Hate (Book II)
A Strike Past Time (Book III)

Friends Always
A Seat at the Table
PRICE TO PAY
The Presence Between

Fit the Crime Series
The Innocence Lie (Book I)
The Identity Lie (Book II)
The Impossible Lie (Book III)

Be On the Look Out for…
The Impostor Lie (Book V of the Fit The Crime series)

**Visit my website, corinnearrowood.com, and register to win freebies
Reviews are appreciated**

About The Author

According to Me:
Local girl to the core. There's nowhere on earth like New Orleans! I am still very much in love with my husband of over thirty-seven years, handsome hunk, Doug. I'm a Mom, Nana, and great-Nana. (four kids, thirteen grands, three great-grands) Favorite activities include hanging with the hubs, watching grandkids' games and activities, hiking, reading, and traveling. I am addicted to watching The Premier League, particularly Liverpool—The real football—married to a Brit; what can I say? I'm living my best life writing and playing with my characters and their stories. I'm a Girl Raised In The South (G.R.I.T.S.) Perhaps the most important thing about me is my faith in God. All of my characters, thus far, have opened a closed heart to an open one filled with Light. Some take longer than others.

According to the Editors:
Born and raised in the enchanting city of New Orleans, the author lends a flavor of authenticity to her books and the characters that come to life in stories of love, lust, betrayal, and murder. Her vivid style of storytelling transports the reader to the very streets of New Orleans with its unique sights, smells, and intoxicating culture.